CONTRACT SIGNED

A TRIGGERMAN INC. STORY

MARIE HARTE

CONTRACT SIGNED

A TRIGGERMAN INC. STORY

Three assassins and a...baby?

Noel "Ice" Cavanaugh's method is foolproof. Get in, do the job, get out, melt away without a trace. Neat. Tidy. No mistakes. This time, though, something isn't right. Two somethings. First, a random attack that feels not-so-random. Then he discovers a baby on his doorstep with a note claiming it's his. Unfortunately, the sexy neighbor who found the boy first has too many questions in her eyes to ignore.

Now Noel has more than one problem on his hands. Splitting baby duty between three badass assassins, figuring out how to fit in more time with Addy...and keeping both of them safe from the danger that's followed him home

COPYRIGHT

ISBN-13: 978-1642920253
Contract Signed
Copyright © 2017, March 2019 by Marie Harte
No Box Books
Cover by Sweet 'N Spicy Designs

http://marieharte.com

ONE

Bangkok, Thailand

The hotel suite, fashioned with expensive furniture, 800 thread count linens, and five-star cuisine sitting on a marble-topped table, was impressive. The guest...not so much.

An older man with dark skin and beady eyes, wearing a military uniform that hung on his skeletal frame, asked in accented English, "What, asshole? Why you here?" He glared, his indignation at being interrupted from his entertainment obvious.

On the bed, a half-dressed female with a vacant gaze lay drugged out of her mind, her age questionable at best. She could have been anywhere from twelve to twenty-five, but knowing this deviant, Noel would guess her to be on the younger end of that spectrum.

He didn't get angry. Instead, he remained focused on the

mission. Cold inside and out, he answered, "My mistake, sir."

"You damn right it is." General Jackass loved being waited on, and he loved even more bullying all the *farangs*—the white foreigners—working in the hotel. "Wattana," he called for his guard outside. "Come. We have intruder."

Not worried in the slightest, Noel bowed low as he backed away, then withdrew his Jericho 941 from his jacket. He straightened, aimed, and squeezed the trigger. So gentle, so perfect... The 9mm round found its target—right between the eyes of the self-promoted general with plans to rape, rob, and pillage his way across a remote border highland in Burma to take over rival opium lanes.

Some dickhead in D.C. had decided to shake hands with this egotistical maniac because his reelection campaign needed the money. Apparently, Senator Cleary had over-looked rumors of child abuse and murder in his quest for reelection funds.

Noel had requested to terminate the good senator, but he'd drawn the short straw, stuck with the general while Deacon took care of the dirty politician. Noel glanced at the deceased drug peddler slumped on the floor, the camou-flaged uniform making the body appear like the stain he'd been in life. "General" Sarawut Mookjai had no redeeming qualities whatsoever. Hell, the guy had even kicked a dog on his way into the hotel.

Noel checked the body for vitals. Once satisfied there were none, he took a photo with his phone. After he sent it off, he straightened his spotless server's uniform and glanced around.

Ah, yes, the girl. He made another quick call to his contact in the city and arranged for her safe passage and detox, if she wanted it, far away from here.

Then he waited, and hearing nothing, proceeded with the plan.

As expected, no one had responded to Mookjai's order, or the silenced hit.

Noel tucked away his gun, then walked out into the hallway. He passed several dead guards as he made his exit from the scene. The hotel boasted twenty-four levels, and only those with Mookjai's personal access could step foot in the sole elevator leading to the top floor. Since Noel had taken care of the security cameras earlier, he didn't worry about being fingered for the hit.

He took the stairs, ignoring the itch at his temple. The wig didn't fit right, and the glue used to adhere the stupid mustache over his lip was just as bad. Freakin' Joe and his "I know a guy who knows a guy" method of acquiring supplies. Hell, Noel had no qualms about paying for quality camouflage out of his own pocket, but his handler was a stickler for protocol.

"On the job, the Business pays for everything," he could almost hear Big Joe reciting, the guy's personal mantra. Because someone had to keep a record of events best kept unrecorded.

Yeah, it still made no sense.

He whistled to himself as he continued down the stairs, his hotel staff uniform as clean as it had been before the job. Once in the basement, he ducked into a closet to change back into his regular clothes. He tucked the uniform into a suit bag, then left as unobtrusively as he'd arrived.

SEVENTY-TWO HOURS LATER, standing in an alley in Seattle, Washington, Noel stared in confusion at the dead guy on the ground who'd tried to stab him with a needle seconds earlier. The needle intended for Noel stuck out of his assailant's neck.

He punched in a familiar number on his phone.

Big Joe answered right away. "What's up?"

"I think someone tried to kill me."

"You *think*?" A low chuckle. "Someone's always trying to kill you. And?"

"And I'm stateside. In Seattle. In public." Well, technically in public, though he stood in a darkened alleyway near the market. Since it was just past seven, and at this point in September the sun set earlier, he didn't overly worry about onlookers.

But this made no sense. Why come after him in the States when his death overseas would be a minor blip on anyone's radar? For that matter, *who* would come after him in the city? The job in Bangkok had gone off without a hitch, his cover uncompromised. And as far as he knew, no one held a grudge against him, because no one but Big Joe and a handful of others knew about the work he did. Noel was slick and silent. They didn't call him Ice for nothing.

"So you almost got mugged. So what?"

"It wasn't a typical mugging." Noel frowned. "No guns or knives. The guy tried to take me out with a hypodermic needle."

"A needle? Was the guy on medication? Or maybe some drugged-out whacko out to score?"

"No. He was fully cognizant. He *looks* like a meth head—a little too much. I'd swear this guy was playing a part, not the real thing."

"Hmm." Big Joe sounded interested. Finally. "Shoot me his photo and prints, and I'll do some digging."

Noel took the dead guy's forefinger and thumb and rolled them over his phone, then sent the electronic prints, along with a photo.

"Be good, boy." Big Joe's trademark signoff as he disconnected.

Noel didn't want to be overly alarmed, because his assailant looked like a tweaker and smelled the part. Nevertheless, he had a feeling this was no ordinary robbery. No drug addict shakedown gone bad. The assault had been sloppy, but the perp looked way too kempt under the grime covering his body, and the method screamed professional.

Besides, what druggie would waste his own drugs in an effort to score more?

Tired, annoyed, and now frustrated that he'd ruined his own homecoming, Noel tidied up the crime scene before leaving. He did his meditation on the go as he headed for the ferry. While keeping one part of himself always on the alert, he let the rest of his mind drift into that calm, kill-free state, knowing he headed *home*.

The one place on Earth that made him feel human.

AN HOUR AND A HALF LATER, his head throbbing, Noel stood in Bainbridge Island, Washington, on the front porch of his Craftsman-style home. In the thick of the woods. Away from people.

Well, *most* people.

He stared at the mess on his doorstep. Or rather, at the mess in the arms of the most annoying woman on the planet.

"I can't believe she'd just drop him off like that." Adeline Rose blinked her bright green eyes at him and shrugged a strand of blue-black hair off her shoulder. She shifted the bundle in her arms, letting the whimpering baby settle over her generous breasts.

A wave of disappointment crushed him, though he

shouldn't have cared that his neighbor had apparently given birth since the last time he'd seen her. She hadn't looked pregnant four months ago, but he'd been in a rush to get to the Sudan for an assignment. So who knew?

Adeline blinked at him, her plump lips parting in question.

As usual, the sight of his neighbor dumped his thoughts straight into the gutter. She had a half-Japanese father, who'd given her a lean build, porcelain skin, and a slight slant to her eyes. Cat eyes. Sexy eyes. From her mother she'd inherited her curves, at least part of her intelligence, and that mouth. He'd had dreams about Adeline Rose's soft red lips...

All the meditation he'd done on the ferry, his sense of peace—gone.

She said something else, and he tuned her out, trying to be just another guy on vacation, any other businessman on a break from a chaotic job that was stressing him the hell out.

"...your baby, and I couldn't help..." she continued in that husky voice that aroused him every time he heard her.

Adeline Rose or "Addy" had been a thorn in his side since she'd moved into her parent's old house two years ago. His only neighbor for half a mile, close enough to borrow a cup of sugar, but he couldn't see her place past the fence, trees, and a spot of distance he liked to think of as his Addy buffer zone. Yet she made her presence known whenever she so much as twitched.

Unfortunately, Noel had a healthy attraction for the nosy woman. Hell. Who wouldn't? Just his type, Addy had intelligence, beauty, and a fierce need to go her own way. He knew almost everything about her, since he'd created a dossier on the woman the moment he'd moved into the neighborhood four years ago. But knowing about her and meeting her in the flesh had proven what a difference reality could make. Words didn't do this woman justice.

He gave her a subtle onceover and wished he hadn't. The sight of her breasts never failed to arouse him, and her ass had given him more restless nights than he wanted to admit.

Then, to have her on his doorstep holding a…

"Wait a minute." He blinked. "*What* did you say?"

Adeline held the infant out to him, and he stared blankly back at her. "He's yours. His mother was dropping him off just as I'd come over to deliver a package mistakenly left at my place."

"What. The. *Fuck?*"

She flinched. "Shh. You'll upset him."

"Upset *him*?" Still, he lowered his voice, staring in shock at the bundle of—joy?—in her arms. "That's a baby."

"Yes. A baby boy," she said slowly. "He's four months old."

"Not yours?"

She sighed. "I can see this is news to you. I'm sorry to be the one to tell you, but according to the lady who dropped him off, he's yours. She left a note with his things."

Noel followed her glance to the duffle bag at her feet.

"I'm sorry, but I'm running a little late. I promised Solene I'd help her out with some cleaning at the daycare. If your little guy gets too overwhelming, call Ash Daycare and ask for me."

None of what she said made sense. But she'd already handed him the baby.

He froze, not sure what to do with something so fragile. "Hold on."

She smiled and waved, then left faster than a human being should be able to move. She disappeared down his long driveway. Seconds later, he heard her car drive away.

He didn't know what the hell to do. *A baby?* This had to be some colossal mistake. Noel was no father. He always used protection when he had sex, because he didn't trust anyone. And he hadn't had more than a blowjob or two in months. Nothing full-on sexual since…

He did the math and groaned. Not since Mexico a little over a year ago.

Make that thirteen months ago.

Another whimper forced him to glance down at the baby in his arms. It wore a hat and had a blanket tucked around it.

Not it—him.

"Jesus."

Panic, the likes of which he hadn't felt since his first mission twelve fucking years ago, filled him. Noel had no idea what to do with a baby.

Always in command of himself, if not the situation, Noel forced himself to concentrate. He cradled the child in his arms, knelt to grab the duffle, then let himself inside the house.

The infant seemed to have fallen asleep between one blink and the next, thank God. He put the baby down on the couch and rummaged through the duffle bag. He found a mound of diapers, formula, some baby things he didn't recognize, a locket, and finally a note.

He scanned it and swore silently.

Now he understood. It all made sense. This wasn't *his* mess. At least, he was almost positive it wasn't. This had to be Deacon or Hammer's fault. That trip to Mexico, he hadn't been alone. He'd been with fellow contractors. Not exactly friends, he and his Business associates had bonded over booze, a successful mission, and a need to sink into a hot, lovely woman.

Obviously this woman had gotten Noel confused with the dark-haired Deacon and/or Hammer.

Feeling much more relaxed now that he understood the situation, he centered himself and made some plans. First and foremost, to retrieve his own bag from the front step. Then a shower, unpacking, and figuring out what to do with this baby. How to take care of it—*him*—would be a good start.

He gently scooped up the baby from the couch and took him into his bedroom. He didn't think kids could move much at four months, but what if he put him on the bed and the boy rolled off and broke his neck? Not cool.

No death at home. Not for Noel. And especially not for helpless kids or innocent bystanders. Nope. Noel aimed for the bad guys, and he never missed.

After leaving the baby on a blanket on the floor, he retrieved his things from the front porch and locked the door behind him, resetting the security system. He found his laptop and turned it on before warming up the shower. He'd been gone only a few months, but it felt much longer.

"Too damn long." He sighed. Noel was tired, and he knew things had to change.

A glance at the sleeping baby on the floor made him shake his head. *Nah, not* that *kind of change.*

After Googling how to care for a four-month-old and mentally reviewing the baby supplies on hand, he felt much more confident. Enough to leave the kid sleeping while he showered. He let the water sluice over him and took his time rinsing off the grime from that other world— the one he worked to make a better place—the one he refused to let touch his real home. A haven where he was safe, alone, and happy with his garden and his fantasies about one particular Rose next door.

Once clean and in comfortable sweats, he ordered a pizza and returned to the bedroom to stare at the four-month-old puzzle on his floor.

Noel was a smart man. He could handle a baby. Well, at least until the kid's *real* father came to collect him. He sat down to draft an email to the two suspects and waited for his dinner to arrive.

Not exactly the homecoming he'd expected. But he couldn't complain. Once again, Noel had conquered all obstacles in his path. A baby was no biggie. Neither was Adeline—Addy—star of his erotic fantasies.

He'd give himself a month to decompress before heading out again. With any luck, he'd hand over the baby within the week, avoid his neighbor, and finally organize his garage before the cold weather really hit.

Feeling much better about life, he even tipped the pizza guy more than usual.

Noel snorted with derision at himself for feeling such panic. A baby. Really. How hard could caring for a kid be?

TWO

Addy wiped down another table while Solene wrangled with a new handyman to fix the dryer since her old helper had retired. Addy listened to them haggle back and forth on price versus function, but her mind was on other things this Friday night.

He was back.

Noel "the Mystery" Cavanaugh had returned. Her neighbor of two years had proven himself to be quiet, absent, and, for the most part, coldly polite when in residence. He didn't like to chitchat, had no use for guests, and had she not seen him eyeing her ass that one time, she might have thought him to be gay.

His house always appeared immaculate—he had land-scapers take care of the yard while he was away—and he never seemed to have a hair out of place on that gorgeous head.

She sighed. She'd been infatuated with the man since the

first time she'd seen him. Her parents liked him, mostly because he was never there. They'd moved to Bainbridge to get away from it all, then moved to Scotland two years ago to take care of her grandmother, where they fell in love with the village and the people.

Addy had happily moved into their home, treating it as her own. Not paying rent helped stretch her paycheck, which was minimal at best on a teacher's salary. But she loved her kids, loved teaching, and loved not having to work summers.

"You going to wipe the varnish off that or what?"

Addy flushed and glanced up at her good friend Solene. "Sorry. A little preoccupied tonight."

"Oh?" Solene sat next to her on a tiny chair meant for preschoolers. "What's up?"

"He's back."

Solene blinked. "*He*, as in, Secret Agent Cavanaugh? Stripper to the Stars Cavanaugh? Ultimate Thief Cavanaugh? Or are we calling him Naughty Noel now? Because personally I'm going with the stripper persona. It's more fun."

Addy sighed. "I wish. Apparently, he's Daddy Cavanaugh now." She explained to Solene what had happened, ending with, "The weirdest thing was that the woman didn't stick around. I mean, wouldn't you *want* to see your child safely with his father before taking off? For all she knew, I was a psycho stalker. A white slaver. A baby killer. A—"

"Okay, I get it. But for all *you* know, she and Daddy Cavanaugh didn't end well, and she wanted a smooth hand-off. Or she was afraid to tell him about the little guy. You said he seemed shocked about the baby."

"He did. I felt bad for him. But it was the first time I've seen him have a personality, so that was kind of neat. He's apparently not a robot. He even said 'fuck'."

"First they say it, then they do it." Solene crossed her fingers. "You go, girl."

Addy laughed. "Yeah, right."

Solene knew about Addy's hopes and dreams. The pair confided in each other, best of friends since Solene had moved back to the island a year ago. They'd been the only two people under the age of sixty in an old monster movie marathon at the local theater and bonded over a lively discussion about Mothra versus Godzilla.

"Seriously though," Solene continued. "What's the deal with your love life? I feel out of the loop. We haven't talked since last week."

Addy sighed. "I saw Brent on Saturday. We went to dinner." The highlight of her evening had been the butter rolls and salad.

"Brent the barber?"

"No, that's Brian. Brent the CPA."

Solene winced. "Oh boy. You really are in a drought, aren't you?"

"Unlike you." Addy envied Solene's easy way with men. Hell, her easy way with life. "I've never met anyone as self-confident as you. What's your secret?" *Besides being a blonde bombshell and former model?*

"I don't give a rat's ass." Solene grinned. "I've seen 'em all. The handsome, the ugly, the fat, the thin, the alpha types, the nerdy geeks. Men are men. Meaning, they all want something for nothing."

"That's a little harsh."

"But true." Solene shrugged. "Hey, I'm happy. I don't need a man to complete me. Honestly, I hire out what I need."

Addy raised a brow.

"Oh, not for sex. I can get that easily enough. I'm talking about fixing pipes or moving furniture. Hell, I had some guy stop to help me fix my tire last month, and I wasn't even trying to flag down help." Solene grinned. "I was wearing a pair of shorts and a T-shirt. What can I say? Men like blondes and boobs, and I'm both."

"A boob?" Addy teased. "Come on, Solene. Not all men are that bad." She'd started to worry about Solene. Her friend had ended a relationship and moved back to Bainbridge, but that negativity over men had yet to change.

Unlike Solene, Addy wanted to love and be loved. She wanted intimacy with a man to be more than a one-night stand. Sex, for her, had always been about more than her body, but her heart and mind as well.

Solene playfully knocked her in the arm. "You're such a goof. A romantic goof. Stop looking at me like you pity me. I can hate on men all I want. Did you see how easy it was to get the maintenance guy to back down the price?" She snorted. "I stuck out my chest an inch more and he knocked the fix-up down to parts only. The labor's free."

"You don't think much of men, do you?"

"No, frankly, I don't." She eyed Addy with interest. "You do, though, don't you?"

"Men are okay."

"Brent is boring. Noel is hardly around, and when he is, he's antisocial. John dumped you when you wouldn't put out on the first date. Mitch left you for that skank Melinda —but good riddance I say. Should I go on?"

"Sadly, no. But Bainbridge Island has a small dating pool. I'm thinking about signing on with a dating site and meeting some people from Seattle too."

"Good luck with that. Talk about crazies…"

"They can't all be that bad."

"Yeah, right. I bet you twenty bucks that before you know it, your Mr. Cavanaugh, the same guy who barely gives you the time of day when he's here, will be on your doorstep with a big smile needing baby help. Once you give it to him, you'll be watching the kid while he's out doing God knows what. Then he'll be gone again, and you'll still be alone."

"I'll take that bet." Yet as she helped Solene clean the rest of the room, she wondered.

The weekend flew by in a flurry of chores and baking for the PTA fundraiser. Addy already loved her new batch of fourth graders. Thank God they seemed much better behaved than last year's hell-raisers. She had a great feeling about the school year, and for once, the weather had stayed sunny and bright through Sunday evening.

But throughout her time spent cooking and cleaning, she kept an eye on the front door and her cell phone near her at all times.

Nothing.

Noel hadn't tried to contact her for anything. She wondered if he'd left the island again. She thought he worked internationally. Something that accounted for all the traveling he did, as evidenced by the tags on his suitcases. She was never sure about his schedule, though she did occasionally overhear people talking about him.

Noel was a popular topic in town. So quiet, polite, and drop-dead handsome, he raised curiosity in the locals. Mostly in the women, she had to admit. But what woman wouldn't be intrigued by a gorgeous man cloaked in shadow? Heck, he barely made any noise when he moved. Everything about him seemed to whisper.

Except he'd shouted the word "fuck". And he'd held a baby in shock.

Monday rolled around, and she got down to educating. The day passed with ease. Still no word from Noel.

Maybe he'd been so overwhelmed with the baby he'd been unable to call for help. Or he felt that since they never spoke much, he had no right to call her.

And I should stop worrying so much about a man who doesn't want to talk to me. Addy felt stupid for being so concerned. Noel had never called her before, never talked to her unless she instigated a conversation, and never seemed to care what she did as long as she stayed away from him.

Unlike the impression Solene had of her, Addy wasn't dying for a man. She had a healthy respect for herself. Just because Brent and Mitch didn't suit her, didn't mean some other terrific guy wasn't out there waiting.

Screw Noel Cavanaugh. Addy was pretty and smart. She'd find a man who at least liked her company.

TWO DAYS LATER, she couldn't take the curiosity anymore. Noel hadn't called. Sheila at the hardware store and Julie at the grocery reported no sign of her reluctant neighbor either. Not that Addy was keeping tabs, but she'd happened to mention seeing him to her friends. And they, as fixated on the mystery of him as Addy, had been on the lookout for him with no results.

"I am such a moron." She grimaced down at the plate of

cookies she held and rang his doorbell. *This isn't about him. It's about the baby. It's perfectly fine to be concerned about an innocent little boy. Besides, his house is amazing on the outside. Nothing wrong with wanting to get more than a peek of the interior.*

The lovely one-level Craftsman looked like it should have graced the cover of a home and garden magazine. White with dark red shutters, an oak wraparound covered porch, a pristine lawn surrounded by landscaped flowers and shrubs, the place looked like a poster for the perfect American family. The only thing it lacked was a mother and two point five children.

Make that one point five, she mused.

The home had to be close to three thousand square feet in size, if not more. Plus, his attached three-car garage and all that space behind the house. Who knew what was out there?

She glanced back at the SUV in front of one of the garage doors and frowned. Noel typically parked his car out of sight, and the vehicle she'd seen in the driveway a few days ago had been a dark gray Mercedes.

That she knew that about him embarrassed her all over again. How pathetic that she paid so much attention to the man, and he could barely stir himself to wave if he saw her.

She decided to leave when the door opened.

"Hel-*lo*." A roguish stranger with short, black hair and

gray eyes smiled down at her. The guy looked taller than Noel, and unlike her neighbor, he actually seemed to enjoy seeing her there on the doorstep.

"Um, hi. I'm sorry to intrude. I just wanted to drop off some cookies for Noel and see how the baby was doing."

"Come on in. I'm Deacon."

She flushed. "I'm Addy. Here." She handed him the cookies and let him tug her into the entryway. He closed the door behind her, and she gaped at the interior.

The black ceramic floor of the entry melded into dark brown hardwoods throughout the open floor plan. She spared a glance for Noel, who was arguing with a giant of a man over a spacious kitchen island. Knowing she'd likely never get another look at the inside of the house, she quickly took it all in. The leather furniture, crafted wooden built-ins, and landscaped paintings on the walls left an impression. She felt gauche and uncultured by comparison.

No wonder Noel had seemed to look through her the few times they'd met. He probably thought he was better than her because he had more money. A look at his house made her think he definitely outclassed her—money-wise at least.

Heck, her house had bits of her childhood artwork on the walls. Family photographs and cute-but-homey décor gave the house a warm feel. Nothing sophisticated or richy-rich, not like this place.

She tried to ignore not feeling good enough to breathe

Noel's air—*You're more than your paycheck, Addy, so much more*—and glanced around for the baby.

"Where's the little guy?" she asked.

"Noel Junior?" Deacon said with a grin.

"Still not funny," Noel growled from her right.

She couldn't help being startled. She hadn't heard or seen him move. "Are you doing okay with the baby?"

He nodded. "It took minimal research to figure out how to care for an infant. He's high maintenance, but not too difficult to handle." *Not like you*, his gaze seemed to say.

"Noel, my man." Deacon's eyes gleamed with mirth. "Addy brought cookies. I think I'm in love."

Addy did her best not to blush, but Deacon's flattery soothed that part of her that worried she'd never be enough for a man. Her pathetic dating life aside, being friends with Solene would be hard on any woman's self-confidence. How easy to pale in her beautiful friend's shadow.

"I didn't mean to disturb you," she said to Noel.

He didn't seem pleased to see her in his home. She swallowed a sigh. Time to forget about Noel and focus on getting a life of her own, away from men who didn't like her. "Is your son doing okay?"

The giant by the kitchen island laughed and sauntered over. "Little Noel is good."

"Shut it, Hammer," Noel said, his voice cold enough to freeze hell over.

The large one named Hammer ignored him. "Addy, is it?" He took a cookie from the plate. "Oh man. Chocolate chip. My favorite." He gently drew her with him into the living area. "Thanks. The little guy is fine." He nodded down to the blanket on the floor, where Noel Jr. rocked on all fours and gurgled.

She melted and knelt by him. "Oh my goodness. You are too cute." She smiled at him, enchanted when he smiled back at her. *Someday I'll have a baby of my own. A husband, a big family with the works: kids and pets and love.*

She stroked the baby's dark hair and sighed. Time to stop daydreaming about her mystery neighbor and get on with her life. The baby seemed fine. Noel had guests. Time to go.

She stood and found him right beside her. Off balance, she took a step back and nearly tripped over a large bouncy ball. But Noel caught her and frowned down at her.

His large hand remained on her waist and sent tingles up and down her spine.

"I guess I'll head home now." Her face felt hot. Geez. This guy turned her inside out. It was more than time to go. "Enjoy the cookies."

He still hadn't let go.

"Noel?"

JESUS. Not only did the woman turn him on just by breathing, she could bake too. The cookies Hammer and Deacon were wolfing down smelled delicious. But not as good as her.

"Save me a few," he ordered, unable to look away from a blushing Addy.

"You can let me go now, Noel. I'm not going to fall."

Deacon snickered. Hammer cleared his throat.

Much as he didn't want to, Noel released his hold on her narrow waist. "Sure." He didn't step back, though.

She did. "Ah, I should go."

"Not yet." Noel felt frustrated. He'd been doing his best to get along with Thing 1 and Thing 2, but the idiots weren't helping. Neither guy would admit to being the baby's father, though they acknowledged what a great time they'd had in Mexico. The DNA results they'd sent in to a special lab would take a few weeks. Until then, he refused to let the guys go home.

The baby was *not* his problem alone. The dirty diapers, the feedings, the constant crying—they were annoying but bearable. The kid's adorable smiles and laughter, admittedly, warmed that coldness inside him without even trying.

The two assassins crowding his private space, invading the schedules and normalcy of his home, however, gave him constant headaches. He'd ached to shoot at least one of them ten times a day, and they'd only arrived forty-eight hours ago.

He wouldn't have minded Addy dropping by before now, and that surprised him. He'd actually wanted to go next door several times over the past few days, to see her pretty eyes and watch her smile. Silly, but the baby was making him feel more human than he liked to admit.

At least with Hammer and Deacon in residence, he wouldn't be stuck playing babysitter forever. No matter how cute the kid was, a baby wouldn't fit Noel's lifestyle. Nor would a sexy, innocent neighbor who was looking way too good in that sweater and jeans.

Remember, Noel, she's too good for you. Way out of your league.

"Hey, Addy, how'd you like to grab some dinner sometime?" Deacon asked out of the blue.

Noel should have poisoned the playboy years ago. He glared, his control once again shot to hell. "She can't."

"I can't?" Addy sounded confused.

"She's got a date with me later."

"I do?"

He nodded and guided her toward the front office, where he pulled them both inside then closed the door. Now standing with her in a smaller space, just the two of them, alone, he felt himself relax.

"Um, Noel? What's going on?"

She didn't appear pleased. *Crap. Probably should have asked her out instead of ordering her.*

"I was thinking you and I could get dinner tonight, if you're free. I'd like to thank you for being so nice about the baby."

She blinked. "You don't need to take me to dinner for that."

"I'd like to." He'd like to do *more* than dinner with her, but complications arising from sex wouldn't work in his favor. Still, even knowing that, he couldn't stop thinking about how he'd take her.

She turned pink again. "Well, I don't know…"

"Think of it this way. We've lived next to each other for two years and I know next to nothing about you." A lie. He knew everything about her…on paper, at least. And that was part of what scared him, his fascination for a woman with a background and lifestyle so different from his own.

"Whose fault is that?" she retorted, surprising him with a bit of backbone. "I've tried to be friendly."

Addy had always seemed so pleasant, even a bit meek around him. He liked her sudden bite. A lot. "My fault entirely," he admitted. "I'm always traveling, and when I get home, I'm so tired I'm normally not at my best."

She bit her lower lip, and he swallowed a groan. "You *are* pretty crabby. But it doesn't help that I probably seem pushy. It's just that we're neighbors, and I was hoping we could be friends. But Noel, we don't need to go to dinner if you don't want to. I swear the cookies was the last time I planned to bug you. I really did just want to see the baby."

She was giving him an out. An easy way to avoid her. Yet he kept seeing Deacon flirting with her in his mind's eye. "No, really. I've wanted to ask you out for a while, but since I'm always gone, I didn't want to seem friendly then aloof when I left again."

"So why the change now?"

Yeah, why? "Because I might be sticking around longer." A truth he hadn't wanted to admit, even to himself. The job was wearing on him. He found himself wanting to extend his stays at home more often than not.

"Oh." She gave him a tentative smile. "Okay then. When did you want to go out?"

"How about tonight? Six-thirty? I'll come over to your place and we can take my car into town."

"Sure." She smiled wider. "I'd better go. See you later." She left before he could add anything.

Always quick on the exit, that woman.

He followed her out into the living room, only to watch the front door close behind her.

"So," Deacon said.

27

"So," Hammer repeated. "She's got great...cookies."

"I'm such a fan of her...chips," Deacon added, trying not to laugh.

Noel glared. "You two are about as mature as a couple of fourth graders." Like one of Addy's students. He knew all about his neighbor, including the fact she didn't do subterfuge. Addy was just as she appeared, an elementary school teacher, currently single, no pets. She relied on her friendship with Solene Hansen to fill her lonely nights, when she wasn't having dinner—and nothing else—with Brent Morgan.

That prick.

"What's the deal with the sexy neighbor?" Deacon wanted to know. "You sure as shit didn't want me going out with her. But from what we know, you live like a monk."

"Sad but true." Hammer sighed. "Dude, get a life."

"Firstly, don't call me dude."

Hammer cocked his head. "Firstly?"

"Secondly, I *have* a life. One devoted to my job, my passion for gardening—"

"Are you thirty or seventy?" Hammer guffawed. "Gardening? Like shoveling dirt over potatoes or dead bodies?" He laughed harder at his own joke. "The bodies I understand. I—"

"*Gardening,*" Noel reiterated, doing his best not to grab

the Jericho hidden under the back of his sweater and shoot Hammer with it, "and—"

"Nights filled with research on your lovely single neighbor. Don't ask." Deacon held off the obvious question. "I hacked your computer. You are seriously stalking that woman, Noel."

Noel felt his cheeks heat. "I am not. I just like to keep tabs on those around me. As a *safety* precaution. Tell me you don't do the same."

"Sure we do," Hammer agreed. "But if my neighbor looked like her..." He thumbed at the doorway. "I'd have taken her out for dinner and a lot more from day one."

"Some of us can keep it in our pants." A burble caused them, as one, to look over at the baby now crawling toward them. "Then again," Noel added, "some of us can't."

Deacon rolled his eyes. "He's not mine."

"Not mine either," Hammer said.

"I know for a fact he's not mine." Not unless that gorgeous woman he'd met at that cantina in Mexico had been poking holes in his condoms when he hadn't been looking. Not likely, considering Noel always kept track of his possessions.

"Sure thing, Noel." Deacon didn't sound as if he believed him. But that didn't bother Noel, because he didn't believe

Deacon or Hammer either. "I still think we need to give the little guy a name."

Hammer shook his head. "That's the dad's responsibility."

"And the mom's." Noel took the locket from his pocket, the same locket he'd found in the baby's duffle bag. Inside the locket, where he'd expected to see a picture of the mother or the baby, were a line of letters and numbers on one side and a name on the other. *X6TFL* and *Angel*. "Any luck on running this yet?" He held the locket toward Deacon.

Deacon sighed and picked up the baby tugging at his leg. "Nothing. I even hacked the Business files." He held the kid like a football, and the baby grinned and waved an arm around. Deacon smiled down at him and continued, "Nothing there either, unless one of us slept with the notorious Angel and didn't know it."

Angel—one of the Business's top contractors. Or what other people called assassins.

Hammer frowned. "No one's ever seen her and lived to talk about it." He paused with a look at Noel. "Then again, not many have ever seen Ice." He turned to Deacon. "Or the Shadow and lived either. Well, except for the three of us and Big Joe."

Every contractor who worked for the Business had a designation. Noel was Ice. Deacon, a thief, was appropriately named Shadow. And Hammer, no surprise, was the Destroyer. Hammer, Deacon and Noel knew each other from a few jobs they'd worked together, and they shared a common handler—Big Joe.

Angel had worked for the Business before she'd departed a few years ago. Big Joe had been her handler too. He'd once let slip that she'd done a few jobs for him before he'd taken on the firm's most successful contractors—Ice, Shadow, and Destroyer.

Joe had also mentioned that she'd left, but not *how* she'd left. Business employees didn't typically just up and quit. Noel had always assumed she'd been killed on the job.

But what if she hadn't?

Hammer pressed the point home. "I did some digging yesterday. Rumor has it she's not as gone as we once thought. Angel is alive and kicking. Or at least she was six months ago."

"Could it really be that simple?" Noel wondered. "Angel is this kid's mother?" According to the note, she didn't plan to return. Ever. So the baby belonged to his father. Noel's head buzzed with the questions constantly brewing.

"Why not?" Deacon said. "But I'm telling you right now. The woman I slept with in Mexico was no contract killer."

Hammer seemed perturbed. "You sure about that?"

"Pretty sure."

Noel nodded his agreement. "Yeah, me too." The woman he'd slept with had been a seductive local. No Mata Hari in disguise.

But Deacon didn't sound so positive, which made Noel think. If one of them had slept with Angel, would he have known? She would have appeared nonthreatening. Sweet, sexy, the perfect bed partner.

Shit.

And the plot thickened.

THREE

A ddy had thought for sure Noel would cancel their date. She half hoped he would. After all her good intentions to finally let him go and focus on finding a decent man to spend time with, one who would *like her*, for God's sake, she'd agreed to go to dinner with him.

Solene thought it hilarious that Noel was playing to type and demanded her twenty dollars the moment the guy asked for babysitting services—no doubt during appetizers. But Solene didn't seem to understand. Noel hadn't and wouldn't ask Addy for help with anything. When he'd asked her to dinner, the invitation had seemed to surprise him as much as it had her.

She didn't think he was setting her up for anything tonight. No laying a grand seduction to get himself a full-time nanny. Solene didn't agree, but then, Solene had trust issues.

"This is nice," Addy said as they sat across from each

other in Mermaid Kitchen, a new high-end restaurant just a short distance from the ferry. Small tables, each lit by candlelight, were adorned with a small bouquet of fresh flowers. The soft jazz playing overhead added to the low key yet no doubt high cost of the dining experience. All the wait staff wore black with aquamarine polo shirts, and they'd all memorized the menus, the wine menus, and could explain, down to the ingredient, what all went into the dishes.

Noel nodded. "I came here a few times this past summer for the food. They have nice quiet tables in the back."

"Oh." She liked to eat out, when she could afford to. This restaurant supposedly had terrific food but could be on the pricey side. Sadly, her recent spate of dates hadn't been keen on forking out a lot of money if she hadn't planned on sleeping with them up front.

I really do need to find a better class of man to go out with.

Realizing that Noel didn't necessarily fit that bill took some of the enjoyment out of the evening. She decided to treat this like an interview instead. With any luck she'd learn something about her mysterious neighbor.

After a moment of silence, Noel jumped into conversation. "You've lived here your whole life, right? Except for your time at college in Spokane."

She blinked at him.

He shrugged and took a sip of water. "Your parents mentioned you once or twice. I was sad to see them go."

"Probably because *they* never bothered you," she said out loud when she'd meant to keep that to herself.

He gave her a rare grin, which lit up his brown eyes and turned them golden.

She blinked, her heart racing at the transition of coldly handsome Noel to warm, out-and-out gorgeous Noel. Amazing what a hint of humor could do for the man. She wanted to touch his mouth, to see what that smile felt like under her fingers. Or better yet, her lips.

Focus, Addy!

"Well, your mom and dad never made me any cookies," he continued, "but your dad's a hell of a gardener."

She nodded, doing her best to regulate her pulse. "He brags about his cucumbers more than he does about me." She smiled. "He and mom are considering staying in Ballater, in Scotland. My grandmother, my mom's mom, is from there. Plus, my dad is a golf nut, and they have a big time golf club there. Keeps him out of mom's hair, and she can bond with Grandma again." She paused. "What about you? Where's your family?"

He was about to answer when the waiter arrived to take their order. After they selected their meals—he declined any alcohol, she noted while agreeing to a glass of wine—he answered, "My parents died when I was young. Car accident. I don't have any relatives that I know of. It's just me."

"Oh." She didn't know what to say. That sounded awfully

lonely. "What about Deacon and Hammer? Are they friends of yours?" *Obviously, you idiot. Why else would they be at his home?*

His lips pinched. "Friends? More like business acquaintances."

The perfect segue. "Speaking of which, what exactly do you do for a living?"

"I'm in finance," he said smoothly. "Deacon and Hammer are too."

"Really? Hammer's into finance?" She could see the suave Deacon talking people into investing in umbrellas for the Sahara. But Hammer? The man looked like his namesake. He was a giant mass of muscle and intimidation, even when smiling around a chocolate chip cookie.

"Hammer's got surprising depths," Noel deadpanned, and she grinned. "But what about you? You're a teacher, right?"

"Yes." She warmed up to the topic. "I teach fourth grade. My favorite subject is English, because I love watching young minds create. My kids are vivid storytellers, and any chance I can hook them on reading, I try." She paused as the waiter brought them their first course then left. "Do you read much?"

"I like biographies and books on gardening."

"I love fiction. Romance, horror, fantasy. Anything, really. I'm a book addict." She scrunched her nose, hearing herself sound as boring as she was. "But I don't just read. I like to do a lot of things." Did breathing or eating count?

He watched her, and she wondered if he found her stimulating, or something to scrape off the bottom of his shoe. She just couldn't tell. "What about you? What do you like to do for fun?"

He sighed. "I'm not that interesting, sadly. I don't party at all hours. When I'm not working, I like to enjoy my downtime with peace and quiet. I'd as much read or garden as stare out at the water and watch the sun set." He grimaced. "I'm told I sound like I'm seventy."

She laughed at his pique. "You think that's bad? The last guy I was dating dumped me because he said I acted like a grandma. I wanted to go out a few times and get to *know him* before I decided to sleep with him, and apparently that's outdated." Realizing she'd overshared, she blushed and hurried to add, "I'm not much better than you in the fun department, I guess. I told you I like to read, but I also paint watercolors and love to hike. I haven't been to a bar or party since college. Not that adventurous for a twenty-six-year-old."

He just looked at her, and all that concentration made her warm in funny places. "Twenty-six, huh?"

Now she felt defensive. "How old are you?"

Another grin. She felt giddy. "How old do you think I am?"

This time it was her turn to stare, but at least now she had a polite reason to do so. "Hmm. That's a good question." Black-brown hair cut short. A tanned face and hands, so he spent time outdoors. He had dark brown eyes that she'd describe more as rich earth than anything chocolatey. Nothing about Noel that would melt. He normally seemed like a block of ice.

Damn if she didn't immediately start fantasizing about what he'd be like thawed out.

For all that he'd asked her out on a date, he hadn't softened much thus far into their evening. If anything, with the exception of those few grins, he seemed even more on guard.

She took in the whole of him: that square jaw, lean cheeks, the rangy body honed by exercise. Not from a gym, she'd bet, but from doing actual work. Running or weight lifting to keep in shape, but not for looks. Vanity didn't seem to fit Noel at all.

"Well?" he asked as the waiter dropped off the rest of their food and drinks.

He had to be a little bit older than her, but not by much. "Thirty-two?"

He smiled. "Not bad. At least you didn't say fifty."

"That would be ridiculous. I'd never go over forty-nine."

He chuckled. An honest-to-God laugh. "I'm thirty years old. But my work in finance sometimes makes me feel older. So yeah, at least thirty-two."

"Ha ha." She smiled back at him. "Do I look twenty-six?"

"Now that's an interesting question."

INTERESTING? How about fascinating, mesmerizing, captivating? She looked edible. Like a sweet dessert he wanted to savor with each lick and nibble, until she was panting and crying out his name as he fucked her until neither of them could walk.

Once again, his thoughts descended to the carnal. *Hell.* The woman wasn't even trying to get under his skin, and she had with ease. He didn't understand it. He'd dealt with killers and seducers, women out to take him for his wallet, his money, for information. He'd been with true beauties, women with culture and genius IQs. Yet none of them had ever affected him like the woman sitting across from him now.

Noel had been attracted to Addy from the moment he'd met her. He liked her parents, and he didn't like many people. The physical attraction made sense; she appealed to his ideal female aesthetic. But digging into her character and "stalking"—as Deacon had put it—for details about the woman had made him want to know so much more.

He'd been smart to keep his distance for so long, taking refuge in the fact he wanted only to be left alone. Because now that he'd taken her out, he was hooked. And Noel and normal didn't mix. His kind of danger wouldn't be good for a sweet woman like Addy.

Then again, there was no danger at home. He'd made it a safe zone. Here, he could play with what-ifs, if only in his mind. Talk about rationalizing, yet...

"What's that look?" Addy asked.

"Hmm?"

"You look like you're about to stab me with your knife." She nodded to the steak knife he'd been gripping.

"Oh, sorry." He came up with a fast excuse. "It's just that I'm trying to say the right thing and not offend you. I have a bad habit of coming across as antisocial."

"No, *really*?" she teased.

Her smile slayed him. Just...

He swallowed a sigh, feeling like a horny, lovesick fool. And wouldn't Hammer and Deacon laugh their asses off thinking of Noel pining over a woman way too nice for him? Damn. Time to sac up and stop thinking foolish thoughts.

Noel didn't do romance or relationships. He occasionally had sex, though he'd never considered himself an excessively sexual man. For him it was a release when the job was getting to be too much. Not like Deacon. The guy would inhale, and on the exhale end up balls deep in a woman. Hell, he'd fucked half of Sicily on that one mission two years ago. *The kid* has *to be his.*

Noel, on the other hand, suppressed his desires the way he did most feeling in his life. Cold, barely there.

Ice.

He gave her a wry smile as he pulled back on his feelings. "See? It's like you know me already."

"I know nothing about you, except that you like gardening, have a baby you insist isn't yours, and live in an amazing house."

"It is something, isn't it?" He took pride in that place, a home he'd bought and paid for with his own money. No handouts or charity, not since he'd turned fourteen and been recruited by the Business.

"But what about you, Noel?" She toyed with her shrimp. "What makes you tick?"

He cocked a brow. "My biological clock?"

"Very funny." She made a face and ate in small bites. So delicate, so dainty while she shot him surreptitious glances. She was being very careful around him, and she set off his alarm bells.

"What?" he said.

"Excuse me?"

"You want to ask me something else. You might as well."

"I'm that obvious?" She shrugged and sighed. "Fine. Not like we can keep dancing around the baby elephant in the room."

He rolled his eyes. "The boy isn't mine."

"Really? He looks like you."

"He looks like Hammer and Deacon too."

She frowned, then her eyes widened. "Oh my gosh. You think one of *them* is the dad?" Then she gasped. "Did you all sleep with the same woman?" She gulped. "*Together?*"

He felt himself flushing, calling on his control as he grit his teeth. "For your information, I do not have sex in front of other people. I'm not into threesomes or foursomes, not into men, and I don't have unprotected sex. Therefore, that baby cannot belong to me."

She had turned beet-red after asking her question, and now she looked mortified, which satisfied him on one level while on another endeared her to him.

Christ, even embarrassed she's beautiful.

Be cold, man. Ice.

"I am so sorry. Sometimes my mouth runs away with me. I read a lot of romance books, so I can get carried away." She buried her head in her hands. "I cannot believe I asked you that!"

He chuckled, which brought her face up. "You're really red right now."

She groaned. "I know. I'm sorry. It's really none of my business, but I figured I'd probably never have a chance to ask you anything personal again, so I'm giving it my best shot now."

He frowned. "What do you mean never have a chance to ask me things again?"

"Come on, Noel. In the two years you and I have lived next door, you've never wanted to be social. Now you have friends—sorry, associates—at your house and a baby, and you don't seem to want any of them there either. The only reason we're even out on a date is because Deacon asked me first." She studied him. "I bet you didn't want me asking him any questions about you, did you?" She seemed depressed, all of a sudden. "As soon as they leave, you'll soon follow, and you and I will be back to square one."

"You have a vivid imagination, don't you?"

"I told you, I read a lot." She ate in the sudden quiet, and he did his best to remain emotionally distant while he took in every detail of her in the candlelight. "I'm just sorry we can't be more than neighbors. But I understand, and I respect your decision to have some space. Let's finish our meals and call it a night, okay?"

Again, another out. But some masochistic part of him refused to take it. "Over a year ago, Hammer, Deacon, and I had concluded some business in Central America. We celebrated—drinking a few *cervezas*—then went our separate ways. We're all dark-haired. The note left with the baby was for the father—who'd had a good time in Mexico. The mother didn't identify herself or name the father. Well, all three of us had been down there. And I *know* that baby can't be mine."

The more he said it, the more he hoped he spoke the truth. He had nothing against the kid, but Noel took his responsibilities seriously. A baby would ruin his preciously scheduled life.

"Oh." She gave him a tentative smile. "Thanks for telling me."

"You're welcome." He put down his fork and knife. "Now, since I told you something about me, you tell me something about you."

"I already told you things about me."

"Why aren't you married with kids already?" A nosy question, but hey, she'd started it, and he wanted to know.

"I haven't found the right man yet."

"Really? I find that hard to believe."

"It's true. The men I've dated have either wanted one thing from me, which they aren't getting until I'm ready for that." A warning he couldn't miss. "Or they want too much too soon. Someday I'd like to marry and have kids, but not after a few dates. Intimacy takes time, commitment."

"I agree."

"It takes a person being there to develop that commitment."

He nodded. "Yes, which is why I hadn't asked you out until now. And for the record, I didn't do it because Deacon asked first."

She raised a brow.

"Don't give me the annoyed teacher look," he warned. "Okay, Deacon asking you out, right in front of me, was a little off-putting. But I never do anything I don't want. I asked you to dinner to spend time with you."

She seemed thoughtful. "So you don't want to have sex with me?"

He hadn't expected such frank talk, but he appreciated her not playing games. "Hell no. I'd *love* that. But I agree that kind of development takes time." *See, this I understand.* Noel liked to make plans, to do things on a time table.

"How much time? Is this where you ask me for a second date and then demand sex?"

He stared at her, his brown eyes so dark they looked black. "Do you talk to all your dates like this?"

BECAUSE IF YOU DO, I understand why you're still single, went unsaid.

Addy didn't know what had gotten into her tonight, but she wanted to see the real Noel again. For a while, he'd been there with her. Then it felt like he'd gone into his head and hadn't come back out. He spoke and curled his lips into the semblance of a grin, but the smile didn't reach his eyes.

He had a clinical way of dissecting conversation, and an almost pregnant pause before he spoke, as if measuring what he gave away. She had seen him blush when she'd mentioned sex, which astounded her. She'd never have pegged Noel to be embarrassed by anything she could say or do. He seemed so controlled and self-assured.

She felt reckless, teetering between wanting to end this debacle or continuing until she took him to bed. One way or the other, she wanted to put an end to her hopeless fascination with the man.

The baby wasn't his? Of course it wasn't. Practical Noel Cavanaugh, financier extraordinaire, would never forget to wear a condom or practice safe sex. He was too buttoned-down to walk on the wild side.

And what a shame, because with a face and seething cauldron of energy like his, Noel had been made to live life on the edge.

He turned the conversation to his many journeys abroad, and she enjoyed the remainder of her safe, if disappointing evening. He certainly had been well-traveled. From Mexico to Iceland to Russia, he'd bounced around the globe working for some investment firm she'd never heard of.

The meal came to an end and Noel paid the tab. She would have offered, but he'd subtly slipped the waiter his card before she could.

"Thank you."

He smiled, yet his eyes remained flat. Did he really think

she couldn't tell he wasn't all here? Why bother asking her out in the first place?

After the waiter brought back his card, Noel drove them to her place, pulling all the way up her driveway to her front door. The night sky had a full moon and bright, twinkling stars. A surprisingly clear night for Bainbridge, and the ideal backdrop for romance had her companion—or she—been so inclined.

She glanced toward his house while they stood on her porch, aware of the thick trees and fence that kept his privacy. Like the man himself, walled off and unavailable unless she scaled his barriers.

If she even wanted to anymore. Solene was right. Men were such a pain in the ass. Too much work.

They climbed the stairs to her front porch and stood in front of her door. No more sexual tension. No awkwardness between them, because she'd have to feel some kind of emotional investment or attraction from her date to get that. And the icy male seemed oblivious to her presence. Like always.

She sighed.

"Good sigh or bad sigh?" he asked, not appearing to care either way. Once again, the man who rarely let an emotion show remained in control.

For her own sanity, she decided to draw the line with him. "You know, I'm just going to be honest with you."

"Please do."

"I think you're attractive. I think you're intelligent." Did he seem to stand a little straighter at that? "But you're emotionally distant and, well, *cold.* It seems a real shame that you're so closed off, Noel. But that's your business. Your life. From now on, we'll be great neighbors, casual acquaintances who might pass each other from time to time, but that's it. I'm sorry if I seemed pushy about getting to know you. You're obviously a private man. And tonight has shown me I should keep my distance."

So disappointing that Noel was bad boyfriend material. But what had she expected?

"What exactly did I do that upset you?"

Again, no emotion in that voice.

Irritated, she glared at him. "You really don't see it, do you?"

He quirked a brow, so patronizing, and said nothing.

Frustrated, because he had so much potential—nice with her parents, lived close by, great income, manners, attractive—she let fly, "I can't do this. You're like a robot, you know? I used to think you weren't even into women before you asked me out. You're so quiet and detached and… Oh, forget it." She opened her door and entered, but when she tried to close it behind her, he stepped inside.

"I have something to say. Then I'll leave."

She should have been frightened by how he'd invaded her

space. But she wasn't. Noel didn't feel like a violent man. Hell, he didn't "feel" like much of anything…warm, mammalian, or human.

She tossed her coat and purse on the couch, then turned and crossed her arms over her chest. "Go ahead."

He stared at her a moment, then walked closer. An odd look entered his eyes, and she knew a moment of uncertainty. "Do I frighten you?"

A normal guy would ask if he scared her. Noel enunciated each word with polite entreaty.

"No." Unnerved maybe, but not exactly terrorized.

He nodded. "Good. You have a valid argument. But there's something I'd like to point out."

"Please do." He was so civilized, so proper. So much handsomeness wasted on someone so…cold.

"I went out with you because I've wanted to for a long time. That much is true. But I think you're equating my sense of control with a lack of imagination."

"I'm sorry. What?"

"I'd like a good night kiss."

"Huh?"

"I'm not asking for sex. I won't put a hand on you. I just want to show you that I'm a flesh and blood man under all my robot armor."

She flushed. "I didn't mean to insult you. It's just that we're so different, and I—"

"One kiss. Then I'll go."

She shrugged and leaned closer, then closed her eyes. "Go ahead."

The things I'll suffer to keep on good terms with my robot neighbor.

FOUR

Noel had never been as out of control as he felt right now. The stubborn, aggravating, self-righteous woman called him *robotic*? Cold, maybe. Self-controlled, sure. But gay? Not into women?

Her lips parted and her eyes remained closed while she waited.

He leaned in and called on his arsenal of seductive weaponry. He'd show her asexual. Noel whispered a kiss over her lips before he thought better of his plan.

Because just a taste of her told him he'd made a slight miscalculation. Her startled breath stopped him, but he didn't back away. Especially when she softened under him.

He gently pushed against her mouth, sliding his lips over hers while fighting the urge to bury his hands in her silky hair. He deepened the kiss, slanting his mouth across hers for better access.

The heat between them felt combustible, a sexual chemistry he couldn't deny. And neither could she, apparently, because she groaned and parted her lips, opening for him.

He slipped his tongue inside, and she teased him, sucking him deeper. His body locked up, his need for her electrifying. God, he ached between his legs, but he'd sworn he wouldn't touch her with more than his mouth.

The kiss deepened, and he stroked inside her mouth, all thought of teaching her a lesson with seduction gone. He wanted nothing more than to hear her moan with pleasure again.

Soft fingers gripped his arms and trailed up his shoulders to curl around his neck.

He tensed and pulled back, staring down at her flushed cheeks and the smudge of black where her eyelashes fanned her cheeks. She slowly opened her eyes to reveal bottomless green depths.

"Not so cold now," she murmured, drew his head down for another kiss, and dragged one of his hands to her waist.

Taking that as an invitation to touch her, Noel held her gently, not wanting to do anything to stop this exploration.

She sighed into his mouth, and he clenched her narrow waist, aware of how much bigger he was than her.

Between one breath and the next, Addy controlled the kiss, suddenly plastered against him while she rubbed against his erection, her soft breasts crushed against his chest.

The last remnants of control left him. Thought took second place behind desire. Behind need. He ravaged her mouth, in command of the situation so he could put her right where he wanted her. He cupped her breasts and pinched her nipples, and she gasped into his mouth.

Then she sucked his tongue again, and he shoved against her belly, on fire to feel her around him.

She moaned and clenched his neck, her nails biting into his skin.

He dragged his mouth down her cheek and blew into her ear, aroused anew when she shuddered and clamped around him like a vise.

"You're mine," he whispered, then kissed and sucked his way down her neck, unable to stop, praying she wouldn't say no.

Thankfully, she met him more than halfway. He felt her small hands at the snap of his jeans and trembled, hoping he wouldn't come before he could get inside her.

He dragged off her shirt and bra while she freed him from his confining pants and underwear. When she put both hands around his girth and pumped him, his eyes crossed.

Fuck me. He nearly came and had to pull her hand away before he embarrassed himself.

She was tugging down her pants and panties while he edged her toward the wall, his pants and underwear pushed down just enough to free his cock.

Her bare back hit the wall, and he lifted her with little effort, putting her where she could do the most good. Before he could bring her over him, she positioned his dick and slid down him like a pole, taking him to the root. *So damn tight.*

She cried out and arched her head back, and he latched on to her throat and started pumping, thrusting faster and harder while she bucked over him, grinding against him with each push and pull.

"Yes, Noel. *Yes,*" she begged. "*More.*"

One hot piece of woman. He could barely think as he rode her harder, desperate to reach that pinnacle drawing so close. Needing to mark her as his in the worst way.

She let go of his shoulders, though he didn't know when she'd put her hands there, and yanked him by the neck down for another kiss.

He devoured her mouth and felt her jerk against him, clamping down as she came. So much heat and that tight grip, and he couldn't stop himself from tearing free from her mouth while he pounded inside her and released, the orgasm so intense he saw black for a moment.

He held her to him, emptying inside perfection while she planted kisses along his cheek and neck, then his mouth once more.

She gentled her earlier ferocity, the tenderness of her touch pushing past the last barriers he'd been holding and making it impossible not to return such gentle regard.

He stroked her hips and ass, gripping her while he finished, loath to pull out.

At that moment, reality reared its ugly head. For both of them.

She blinked, stared down between them in horror, then paled. "You came inside me."

"I—*oh, shit.*"

He was the biggest asshole on the planet. What had he been thinking? All his denials about irresponsibility and how he'd never had sex without protection—which he hadn't until now—shot to hell. So sure he hadn't made a baby in Mexico, and then he tried to make one here?

She scrambled to get down, and he let her, mourning the loss of heat around him while she disappeared down the hall and slammed a door behind her.

He stared in dismay at his still half-hard cock, not sure what had just happened.

Ice never made a mistake. Ice was all control, all discipline. No accidents, nothing random. Yet he'd shoved inside a woman—*unprotected*—and nearly had a heart attack while having the most intense orgasm of his life.

Shaken with what had happened, and why he'd let it happen, he tucked himself back in his clothes and righted his appearance. After washing his face and hands in her kitchen sink, he tried to clear his mind and deal with the problem at hand.

Namely, he might have just given Noel Jr. a baby brother or sister.

Addy joined him wearing a robe that covered her from head to toe. Soft and purple, it looked royal, especially worn around the shoulders of a queen with an axe to grind.

"We—I—you—" She paused, took a breath, and let it out. "I'm not on birth control, but I should be safe. I don't think I'm at the risky part of the month yet."

"Good." The relief that filled him made him light-headed.

"But do I have anything *else* to worry about?" She flushed but met his eyes, and the rosy cheeks and creamy complexion over her face and neck brought his gaze to her chest, and lower. So damn beautiful. "Noel?" she growled.

So his kitten had a bite.

No, not my kitten. She's a mistake, that's all. A curiosity assuaged.

He cleared his throat, still in a daze. "Ah, no. Nothing to worry about. I haven't been with anyone in months, and I always get checked out. Every six weeks, actually. Part of the job."

She nodded, embarrassment taking the place of relief.

"Damn, Addy. I don't…" He had no idea what to say, not sure she'd believe him. He ran a hand through his hair. "I never meant to… I mean, I wanted to kiss you. Sure. The sex was off the charts fantastic. But I hadn't intended for that. Not tonight."

Her eyes had a glassy sheen, and the thought of her being upset scared him. Literally caused his heart to race and his mouth to dry up.

She swallowed audibly but didn't cry, thank God. "It was my fault. I prodded you. I wanted you to...you know."

"Well, it was my fault as well." He felt better sharing the responsibility. She might have started their descent into madness, but he'd sure as hell followed her every step of the way.

They stood there staring at each other, and he couldn't stop himself. He closed the awkward space between them, took her head in his hands, then kissed her. A gradual build-up to the lust remained, and fiery need threatened to consume him again.

He pulled back and wiped his thumb over her lower lip, pleased to see her shiver. But this time he remained in control.

"Not so cold now, am I?" he had to say.

She traced her lips with a finger and shook her head. "N-no." Her eyes seemed nearly black, swallowed up by dilated pupils slaked with lust. "I, ah, I guess you should go."

"I'll be right next door if you need anything." He stared at the robe, knowing now what she hid inside, and did his best to ignore the twitch between his legs.

"Anything, huh?" she answered, not sounding tart so much as worried.

He felt himself smiling. "Anything, Ms. Rose. Anything at all. I'm your man."

Then he left, the taste of her lingering on his mouth, the musk of her still coating his skin. He smiled all the way home, even when Deacon handed him a smelly baby, swore, then darted out of the house.

ADDY STARED in shock at the closed door, still not sure how she'd had sex with her robotic neighbor. Best-sex-of-her-life sex with a cold, controlled man who rarely smiled. One minute she'd tried kissing him off, the next she'd been kissed breathless. Then screwed until she couldn't think.

I let him come inside me. Warning bells, shrieks of disaster, lamentations of stupidity. She swore up and down and raced into the shower, scrubbing herself clean of everything but an unnerving need to see him again.

Good Lord, he'd been the most demanding lover. He'd taken her against her wall like a conquering raider, owning a pleasure slave who wanted nothing more than to—

"Wake up, Adeline! This is not one of your books!"

When even yelling at herself failed to keep her mind off reminders of Noel's powerful pleasure, she forced herself to go to bed, not waking until the next morning.

The day passed in a blur. Her children were thankfully

well-behaved and fun to work with until the bell rang at three-thirty. She watched them leave before cleaning up her room. Then she drove to a nearby coffee shop.

Addy ordered her favorite, a hazelnut latte, and sipped slowly, tucking into her jacket to preserve the heat.

"Hello? Earth to Addy." Solene waved a hand in her face then sat at the picnic bench in front of the shop, sipping from her own covered drink. "Best cocoa in town." She raised her cup to Addy's, and they toasted the crisp fall air.

Solene watched her over the cup, saying nothing, a question in her eyes.

Addy couldn't stand it. "I had sex last night."

Solene didn't blink.

"With a man. With Noel."

Solene's lips curled. "Good to know. I take it he knocked your socks off?"

Addy hid behind her hands while her friend laughed.

"Hey, sometimes we single ladies need human connection. No biggie, Addy, just—"

"We went at it like animals, and we forgot to use protection. So stupid," Addy added in a low hiss.

Solene blinked. "Seriously? You could be the poster child for Trojan, Ms. Responsible Adult. He was that good?"

"He was amazing," she whined. "And right after I'd called him a robot."

"Oh, this I have to hear."

Solene was the perfect venting partner. She listened, agreed with Addy, and offered compassion and understanding.

So why did Addy want to cry?

"I know I'm not going to get pregnant." She kept trying to convince herself. "I'm regular as clockwork, and the timing was wrong for a baby. As scary as the aftermath was, I want to be with him again. And not just for sex. He has all these depths I'm just coming to understand." And she'd called him a robot. "But I don't even know if we'll see each other again after that."

Typical man, Noel had gone and ruined everything. Just when she'd figured to cut him out of her life and move on, he'd devastated her mind and body.

"Now that could get awkward, especially since you live right next door."

Addy narrowed her eyes. "Are you laughing at me?"

Solene chuckled. "Only partly. You finally went for it and grabbed that tiger by his big?—little?—tail."

"Huh?"

"More than six inches?"

"*Solene.*"

"That's a yes, then." Solene nodded. "You turn super red when you're embarrassed, you know."

"Shut up."

"Look at it this way. I doubt Mr. Roboto is used to what happened with you guys either, not from how you described him. So maybe he's as freaked out as you are."

"I doubt it."

"You don't know. You need to talk to him. Just go next door and discuss things."

"I can't. He's got company."

"Chicken."

"Bok bok."

Solene shook her head. "You can handle a classroom full of rowdy nine-year-olds, but one guy scares you. Pathetic."

"Why do *I* have to be the one to discuss it? Why can't he come over and talk to me?"

"You're reaching."

Still, Addy liked that idea much better. She stuck to her guns throughout the evening into Wednesday after school. Noel hadn't called or come over. So maybe their night had been a one-time thing? The thought depressed her, that he'd be like so many others. But she'd decided to stop being the one to run to him. If he was interested, he'd come to her.

Just before she readied to turn in for the night, someone knocked at the door.

She put on a robe and checked through the peephole. The sight of an annoyed Noel holding his—*the*—baby, amused her. She opened the door a crack. "Noel?"

"It's not the mailman," he grumbled. "Can I come in?"

"It's late and"—he pushed his way in—"I guess you're in. Seems to be a habit with you."

He grunted, and she took that to mean any number of things.

"Well?"

"I tried to stay away and give you space, but then the kid keeps crying. Hammer took off and Deacon's been busy. So it's just me with the boy."

"No name yet?" she asked, reaching for and taking the baby before she could stop herself. "Oh, you are so cute." She snuggled him and breathed in the scent of innocence. "Is he dry?"

"What?" Noel appeared frazzled, and she loved that look on him.

"His diaper. Is it clean?"

"Oh. Yes. First thing I check before his royal highness started caterwauling."

She blinked. "Caterwauling? You seriously just used that in a sentence?"

He shrugged. "I've been reading about the English monarchy. Some of the archaic language lingers." He sighed. "I would have talked to you sooner but I've had my hands full. I'd like to go out again."

She hugged Noel Jr.—as she liked to think of him—tighter. He grabbed her hair and cooed, no longer upset while she rocked him against her. "By go out, you mean…?"

To her delight, Noel flushed and shoved his hands in his pockets. He wore a dark green sweater and jeans that looked as if they'd been pressed. She had never, in the two years she'd known him, seen him in anything resembling slovenly attire.

"I mean you and I could go out to dinner again or see a movie. Maybe take a hike."

"Oh." She was disappointed and shouldn't have been. But God, just thinking about how amazing he'd been woke her ovaries from their hibernation.

"I mean, sure, we could sex it up in a bed next time, but I thought you'd like to get to know me better first. You know, so that you feel better about being with such a cold, unemotional man," he delivered in a remote voice.

"Ha ha." At least, she thought he was joking.

The gleam in his dark brown eyes and slight quirk of his lips showed he was. "Or are you a fan of wall sex instead?"

She covered the baby's ears. "Shh. He's too little for this talk."

Noel snorted. "Trust me, that kid's no innocent. He's shoved all sorts of things into his mouth all day. Including one of my favorite silk ties. He's been pooping and crying all day long."

For all Noel's harsh words, he stroked the baby's head with a tenderness that should have surprised her but didn't. She noticed the calluses on his fingers, in particular on his middle and forefinger and thumb. From lifting weights, maybe?

He saw her regard and lifted his hand to her cheek, stroking her there and making her shiver with need. His gratified smirk embarrassed her.

She bit her lip. "You do like control, don't you?"

"I do. I live for it." He nodded. "And that person you're holding is driving me to drink. How can someone that small be so dissatisfied with life? And by all that's holy, how can he stink so badly?"

She laughed at his disgust. "He's been with you for a few days now. This is news to you?"

"Deacon's been handling him, mostly. But he had a project to deal with."

"And Hammer took off," she remembered.

"Right. Which leaves me, but I have to go into the city tomorrow on business." He gave her a look she couldn't decipher. "I'll be done by Friday. Would you like to go out Friday night?"

She said nothing, just watched him.

"In Seattle? I thought we could see a show, if you like."

"A show?"

"A local production of *The Taming of the Shrew*."

Her insides warmed. "Oh, Shakespeare. That would be great."

He paused. "I thought we could spend the evening in Seattle, return on Saturday. A hotel, my treat."

She just looked at him.

He sighed. "Two beds, I promise."

"Well, I don't know."

"Of course, if you don't think you can control yourself around me, I can get us each our own room."

"I can control myself." She hoped. "The question is, can you?"

He took the baby back in his strong arms, and she saw little Noel Jr. curl trustingly into that broad chest. "I'm not the one who escalated that kiss." He just had to remind her. "Or who put her hot little hands down my pants to grab my—"

"Okay," she interrupted and ushered him toward the door. "Text me the details and I'll see you Friday."

"No kiss?" he teased, standing at the doorway.

She pecked him on the cheek, not trusting herself, no matter what she'd said, and gently shoved him over the threshold. She heard him laugh as he walked away.

Despite handing her the baby, he hadn't asked her to help in any other way.

Addy grinned. "Solene, you owe me twenty bucks."

FIVE

He read the report twice, just to be sure, and smiled.

He couldn't have planned it better himself. All three of them together, stateside. Noel and his sentimental attachment to that house. It was a deathtrap waiting to happen. He knew it. Noel knew it. But the bastard didn't think anyone could touch him, that because Big Joe liked him he was too fucking special to terminate.

As if the Business wouldn't execute Cavanaugh on a whim. Big Joe was a real shit. If the guy liked you, you were golden. If not...

Hell, look at Angel. She'd worked her ass off. Done things he'd never have agreed to do. All for the greater good. And then, dropped. Executed for treason she hadn't even committed. The poor bitch had managed to piss off one too many people, him included, but he'd at least have given her a proper send-off. But not the dickheads running the Business. They shot first and asked questions later.

Angel was just more proof that the Business needed new management. Someone with a long range plan who hired better middlemen than Big Joe. Borislav and Meridia were just as bad, but at least they didn't feign respect. They plainly showed their fear and disgust on their faces. Or at least they *had*, until someone had gouged out their eyes and ripped out their tongues.

He grinned. Ah, but he was saving Big Joe for last. No sense in giving away the game too early to the ignorant players.

He read the report once more, then dialed a number on his phone.

His contact answered immediately. "Nine here."

"Nine, put the others in place."

"Roger that. Annette's in play as well."

"Good. Any word on Deacon Shaw?"

"Sorry, sir. We lost him somewhere at the airport. I'm still not sure how he ditched us. Malory was on him."

And Malory was a god when it came to tails. A shadow for *the* Shadow, he thought with curbed amusement. The perfect foil to take out Deacon when the time came. "He'll come back. I'm not worried." But he was curious to know what the hell Deacon was up to. "Hammer still in place?"

"No." A pause while he waited for Nine to continue. "He boarded a plane for Philadelphia last night. He touched down, caught a private transport and met with…well, we can't be sure. But Annette thought she heard mention of Phantom in the area."

"*What?*" That didn't bode well. Phantom didn't play nice with anyone, the government-sponsored Business *or* those in the private sector. An odd choice for a Boy Scout like Hammer to meet. "Dig into that, but do not, under any circumstances, let our involvement get back to Phantom. We don't need that kind of trouble." Not when his plans were coming together so perfectly.

"Yes, sir. Anything else?"

He thought about it. "Activate Wilkes and Rene. They're a go."

Nine chuckled. "Yes, sir."

"That's all."

"Nine, out." Nine disconnected.

He stared at his phone and clicked through to a photograph of Wilkes's younger brother, Ted. He'd warned Wilkes that his brother wasn't ready for their world, but Wilkes wouldn't listen. As predicted, Noel had ended Ted's short-lived life with little effort. And really, who used a cover that poor—a meth head mugging gone bad—and thought he could get away with it?

The only good thing to come from Ted's demise was that Noel had his guard up. Caution made Ice even sharper than usual. Such fun and a true challenge to take the man out at the top of his game. But then, Noel deserved all the payback coming to him.

For Mexico—he'd never forget.

THURSDAY EVENING, Deacon eyed the droopy diaper on Noel Jr. and cringed. Where the hell was Hammer when it mattered? And why send the giant to gather information? If they needed intel, they used Deacon. They needed someone blown up, crushed to death, or out and out annihilated, they sent Hammer.

Or, more correctly, Hamilton Aston Montgomery III. Deacon grinned. What a pansy-ass name. Hammer hated it. Which made it so damn fun to use around the huge killer.

The baby babbled and started tugging at his full diaper, and Deacon swooped in and held the kid at arm's length.

Apparently being dangled so high was fun, because the boy laughed and laughed while Deacon frantically sought the diaper bag.

No joy.

Where the hell did Noel put it? The kid tugged harder, so Deacon darted into the bathroom and set the toddler in the tub. And just in time, because that diaper fell off.

Jesus. Cursing Hammer and Noel to hell and back, he rushed to get a spare diaper and a box of wipes from the baby's room. He heard a shriek and darted back into the bathroom. Just as the baby reached for the dangling wash-cloth turning the shower handle, Deacon put his body between the kid and the ice-fucking-cold water that followed.

He shut off the water, too late to save himself, and stood the dirty baby in the tub while he wiped the boy clean with a washcloth. Then he dried the kid and held him in his arms, staring down at such innocence.

The baby babbled to himself, seeming pleased to be naked. Deacon sighed and sat on the toilet with the kid in his lap, lost in thought.

He wanted a beer. Freakin' Noel and his inopportune meeting to get "information." More like another shot inside his sexy neighbor's pants. Finally, someone had melted Ice's heart, but the timing couldn't be worse. He'd seen Noel acting goofy, had talked to Hammer about it for some time. Meeting the gorgeous Adeline Rose in the flesh made some sense of Noel's fixation. But did the guy's crush need to blossom *now*, when Noel Jr. was in the middle of the runs?

Another God-awful second later, Deacon glanced down to see he should have made putting a new diaper on the kid a priority.

"God damn it!" He stood and held the boy at arm's length. So of course the kid started crying. Deacon wanted to cry too. "This was a new pair of jeans. You could at least have the decency to make Deacon your first word." The baby

71

sobbed some more, until Deacon cradled his stinky ass tight.

The boy blinked big brown eyes at him and stopped crying, finally.

"Dea-con. Dea-con," he repeated, doing his best not to gag at the stench coming from his now-ruined pants *and* shirt.

The baby stuttered what sounded like *Dee*-something. Twice.

Deacon stared. The baby suddenly discovered his toes.

Having learned his lesson, Deacon hurried to clean and diaper the kid. Then he stripped down, cleaned up, and fetched new clothes before he made a call.

NOEL LISTENED to the message with half an ear. Something about shit everywhere and the baby saying *Deacon*. Yeah, right. As if a four-month-old could communicate past grunts and coos. Though the thought of Deacon covered in poop made Noel smile.

He finished gassing up his car, then drove toward Fremont, where he had a meeting with one of Big Joe's informants. He parked and walked across the street, only to hear the squeal of tires and the roar of a fast-moving car. He waited on the sidewalk, out of the way, for the street drama to unfold. But he saw no car chase or reason for the red Mustang to be driving so fast. Or to be veering toward him.

Noel stood in place until the last possible second so the car wouldn't mow him down. Before it hit, he jumped back, avoiding major injury, just a graze and some massively sore muscles from the fender. But man, that had been close. The car fishtailed, righted its trajectory, then sped away as the bright lights of a nearby patrol car gave pursuit.

"Holy shit! Yo, man, you all right?" someone asked him.

Noel rolled to his feet and dusted off his trousers and jacket. "Yes, thanks. Stupid drunk, I'll bet."

Several onlookers nearby started talking about the number of DUIs in the paper lately.

Noel quickly walked away, heading toward his objective and ignoring the pain in his knee where he'd hit the pavement. He entered the café and ordered a bowl of soup and a salad. Then he waited.

Half an hour later, he left his companion and the meal behind. But the nosy individual lurking in the back hadn't fared so well. Big Joe's informant didn't like being spied on. Neither did Noel, but he would have simply put a hurt on the snooping dishwasher. Broken a bone or three.

The informant, however, had utilized a poison that would make itself known in a few hours, wherein the spy—*dishwasher, my ass*—would become violently ill, assuming he didn't end up dead of a heart attack first. The poison would also be untraceable unless someone knew exactly what to look for.

Noel walked back to his car, pulled a subtle diagnostic tool from his pocket, and after verifying the car hadn't been tampered with, got inside. He called Hammer's number, let it ring twice, then hung up and waited.

First, a botched druggie attack. Now, a drunk driver. Two coincidences? Noel wasn't buying it. And just who the hell had put a spy in the diner to watch Big Joe's guy? Big Joe? Someone else from the Business? Some faceless enemy? Questions on top of questions. Since the informant hadn't wanted to wait for answers, just get out of Dodge, and fast, Noel was no closer to knowing anything about what looked like amateur attempts on his life.

Big Joe's run-down of the dead meth head turned up little but the name of a guy who had never crossed the street at anything but a crosswalk. Ted Wilkes. Nothing else.

But who really wanted Noel dead? Big Joe hadn't passed on any warnings about his cover being blown, and the government didn't know who he was or where he lived. Sure, they knew about Noel Cavanaugh, the finance consultant. And Noel Ridgemont, the man who lived in Washington and was on the books for a popular lobbyist. They didn't know Ice. Unless someone in the Business had decided to take him out. He had to wonder if Big Joe was in on it. Or was Big Joe being played?

"Or am I dreaming up conspiracies where there are none?" Noel let out a frustrated groan. If the Business wanted him dead, he'd be a lot closer to nearly deceased. No bruise on the knee, he'd be dodging a bullet to the brain. The puzzle gave him a headache, because he needed to solve the riddle of his accidents before meeting up with Addy. No way he'd do anything to place her in danger.

Unless there was no danger. Nothing but a baby with smelly diapers to contend with until they learned who had fathered the little guy.

Personally, Noel leaned toward Deacon. The playboy with the sly grin and supposed charm liked the ladies. A lot. Deacon might dip his wick in a less than safe manner. Hammer liked women as well, but he seemed more cautious, like Noel.

As if thinking about the guy had conjured him, Noel's phone rang. "Hammer?"

"I talked to our ghostly buddy." To Phantom. Interesting. No one ever saw or heard from Phantom unless he wanted it. And in this instance, Phantom had contacted Hammer.

"What did he want to know? Did you see him?"

"Now you know the guy is all but invisible. We discussed matters online, in a secured but deserted facility I had to be driven to. So much fuckin' drama." Hammer snorted. "But I gotta tell you. This shit is getting downright weird."

"How so?"

"I was hit with a lot of questions about Noel Jr."

Noel blinked. Hammer hadn't planned to ask anything about a baby. Just about that code on the locket and rumors about unauthorized missions. "What?"

"I know. Nothing about the possible attempt on you. We didn't talk about Angel or that code. Just questions about a baby."

"What did you tell him?"

"That the kid was none of his fucking business."

"Not smart."

"I was trying to get a rise out of him. I ended up getting a lock on the location he called from. Before I could enter the hotel, a SWAT team showed up and arrested a major drug dealer. It was crawling with cops, so I waited. When I tracked down the computer on the other end of the server, I found it in a hotel room down the block that had been sterilized. Everything wiped down. Just a black phantom mask left behind on the bed."

"Hell." Phantom's involvement with the kid couldn't be good.

"What do you want me to do? I'm thinking I should come back. I don't like how this is shaking down."

"Me neither." He paused. "I think another attempt was made on me today." He described the attempted hit-and-run.

"Seriously? That's sloppy, Noel. A drive-by. Poison. Getting you alone and plugging you with bullets. That's art. But this? It's rinky-dink, if it's even real. Not Business, man."

"I know." Noel sighed, then asked the question he dreaded broaching, but he wanted a second opinion. "I invited Addy to come out for a Friday night date. Should I cancel?"

"Nah. You can protect her if there really is someone after you. And hell, maybe draw them out so you can ask some questions. Better to fight them in a crowded city than on the island, right? You don't want that shit near your home."

Hammer understood.

"Right." Noel felt a sense of relief he didn't need to cancel on Addy. "I'll be here through Saturday afternoon. Deacon's on point with the kid. You staying or coming back?" He'd almost said "coming home."

"I'll give it another few days then head back. I have something I want to try with our ghostly dude." He paused, then Noel heard the smile in his voice. "I wouldn't rush back if I were you. Deacon left a message on my voicemail, and he didn't sound happy. I gather he's not into changing diapers."

Noel grinned. "No, he's not. But he'd better get used to it. Or you should, come to think of it."

"No way. You can think whatever you want. I didn't father a baby. No way, no how."

"We'll see soon enough, won't we?"

"Fifty bucks says it's Deacon."

"I won't take that, because I agree with you." Noel started up his car. "I know I asked you two not to leave."

"More like ordered us to stay."

"Big Joe isn't giving you a hassle about the time off, is he?"

"Nah. He's plenty busy with the rest of his stable." Hammer paused. "You know Big Joe has a half dozen contractors active and running around at any given time. The three of us being on break is no biggie. And even if he did know we're hanging together, it's not unusual for us, right? He knows we're friendly."

Friendly, but not exactly friends. "I don't know if I like him knowing that." Noel felt uneasy. The Business didn't frown on interoffice relationships, but they rarely dealt with them, the nature of a contractor's work being solitary. "Do you think he has any idea about the kid?"

"Nope. I mean, he *could,* but that would mean he has eyes-on. We know our phones are clean. And we've all been very vague about the situation when communicating. Far as Big Joe knows, we're off doing our own thing."

"I guess you're right." Still, he had a weird feeling in his gut.

"But Noel, these accidents you keep having... Keep your eye out. I'll talk to you when I know more." Hammer disconnected.

Noel grimaced and tucked his phone away, then drove

back to his hotel. He made sure no one followed him. But just to be on the safe side, he switched to his backup hotel, registered under an alias, and rested up for the following day.

He'd need his wits about him to deal with the real danger at hand—Adeline Rose and a shared suite with one big-ass bed.

ADDY CONTINUED to call herself all kinds of stupid for agreeing to a date with a man who made her lose all control. He'd honest to goodness seduced her into sex on the first date without even trying. And then to forego a condom? It was like a sexual Darwin Award for most idiotic or desperate female of the decade.

She sighed, trying not to be too hard on herself. Addy was only human, and she'd had a crush on Noel for years. Add to that she hadn't had sex in over a year and she'd been primed to detonate near Sexy Cavanaugh.

But now that she'd taken the edge off—so to speak—she could better handle herself with him. She liked Noel. When he'd let go of those emotional shields holding him back, he'd showed fascinating layers of complexity. But it was getting through those shields to the core of the man beneath that motivated her to see where her relationship with Noel would go.

As Solene had said, it wasn't like Addy had men breaking down her door. Sure, Brent had called for another dinner date, but she'd pretended to miss seeing the message, returning the call to his business when she'd known he'd be at home.

Brent. Such a nice man. Such a boring man. He owned his own accounting firm on the island. He had steady work, but not many interests outside that of a tax break or football.

Addy *loathed* football.

Talk with Brent had her mind wandering in minutes. As annoyed as she'd been with Noel, she'd never been bored with him. Disappointed, attracted, annoyed, but never bored.

She walked off the ferry with her roller bag by her side and found Noel waiting patiently for her in the terminal. He seemed so still, blending into his environment so well that a few people nearly bumped into him when the crowd coming off the ferry swelled.

He saw her and nodded. A tilt to his head, no smile, but she swore his eyes warmed.

A few ladies near her gave him second and third looks, and she knew what they saw. A handsome, if reserved, man. That look of take-it-or-leave-it-I-don't-give-a-damn that intrigued a girl to pry under that icy exterior.

Down, girl. Remember, you're in control of your hormones now.

She gave him a small smile and took his arm, allowing him

to walk her to the parking lot. He put her bag in the trunk of his car and held the door open for her. A gentleman, and she didn't think he was putting on an act. This was the real Noel behaving as he normally would.

"Thank you."

"You're welcome."

She caught another hint of a smile. Not in his lips so much, but in the slight crinkle of his eyes and the tilt of his head. She should have thought it odd to be able to read him so well, but she found it a challenge to keep up with his near-invisible tells.

"Did your week go well?" he asked, all politeness as he drove them to the hotel.

"Fine, if you don't count one of the boys daring four others to eat their glue sticks. Mind you, these are eight- and nine-year-olds. But three of them ate the glue and got tummy aches. Then there was the parent incensed that her daughter comes home covered in marker every day. Well, I can't control what Becky Crowder does on her walk home. At least she uses temporary markers."

He coughed, to cover a laugh, most likely. "Well. That sounds...interesting."

"What about you? How did your meetings go?"

He sighed. "About as well as your week went. I made very little progress. But at least I was saved from having to change some very dirty diapers."

"Oh, yes, about that. Deacon came over last night in terror. I think Noel Jr.—ah, I mean, the baby," she corrected when he gave her a look, "is teething and not sleeping. Deacon was at the end of his rope. So I introduced him to Solene's daycare. I think he's going to use her for a little break. But don't worry." She hurried to forestall the question following his frown. For all that Noel insisted he wasn't the father, he acted protective at the oddest times. "Solene's an expert. Kids love her, and she has a soft spot for babies."

"Solene Hansen? I think I met her once in town."

"Yes. Blonde, beautiful, with an attitude? That's her." And what did Noel think of the ex-model?

He snorted. "Oh right. The attitude. I remember her now. Good. She and Deacon can work things out." He gave her a quick assessment without revealing his thoughts. "You and I have a date night planned."

She felt tingly as she envisioned their date getting carnal. Because as much as she wanted to prove to herself she was above sex with an almost stranger, she'd never been so pleasured by a man in her life. Already, she felt addicted to Noel's touch. Not good when he'd probably be getting ready to head out again soon.

He patted her on the knee. "Don't worry, Addy. I'll go easy on you."

She ignored the heat left by his touch and placed his large

hand back on the steering wheel. "Whatever, Noel. I think we both know *you're* the one with the control problem."

"Is that so?" He shot her a grin that melted her panties right off. Or at least, that's what her lady parts told her. She felt exposed, aroused, and downright hostile that he could make her want him so easily. *Damn.*

"Yeah, neighbor. That's so," she growled. "Now let's enjoy this platonic date night of ours. That's *if* you can keep it in your pants."

He blinked at her. "Funny, but that phrase has been going around a lot lately."

SIX

The hotel blew her away. Trust Noel to find them deluxe accommodations. He'd booked a suite overlooking the Pike Place Market. A single bedroom suite at the Inn at the Market.

Talk about a sweet suite.

She forced herself not to giggle like a little girl and swallowed her nerves as they returned from their evening out.

"All right?" he asked as they took the stairs to their room.

"Fine."

"I enjoyed our meal, but I think the play was the best part of tonight, don't you?" He strode with confidence in a power suit that he wore with perfection. Dark gray slacks and jacket over a dark gray button up shirt he'd left open at the collar. More than one head had turned tonight watching him.

At least she'd been smart enough to pack a knee-length dress that complimented her figure and coloring. The navy blue sheath had a plunging neckline, long sleeves, and a tiny slit up the left side that looked more classy than slutty. Or so Solene had said.

Personally, Addy would have rather worn dress slacks and a silk blouse, but even she knew she'd have been outclassed tonight wearing that.

He let them inside the suite and locked up behind them.

"Yes," she said, when she realized he waited on her account of the evening. "I'm a Shakespeare fan, but I particularly love his comedies."

"I prefer his histories, but this one was well done."

She could have guessed he'd go for history over comedy, or romance, for that matter.

"I—"

He cut her off by taking her hand in his and kissing the back of it. She stared into his dark gaze, breathless.

"Have I told you how beautiful you look tonight?"

Unable to form coherent words, she nodded.

"Let me tell you again. You look gorgeous. I'm a sucker for dark hair, and yours not only looks like silk, it feels like silk." He ran a hand over her hair, and she felt that touch to her toes. "You know, you're just the right height."

"For?" she somehow managed to say.

"A kiss." He pecked her on the forehead then gave her a sly grin. "How about we play for secrets?"

"What?"

"Blackjack. Winner gets to ask questions of the loser."

"Fine. But you can't lie."

He dropped her hand and put his palm over is heart. "Cross my heart and hope to die."

She grimaced. "Please. I hear enough of that kind of talk at work."

He chuckled. "Me too."

When she would have asked him about that, he told her to get comfortable and meet him on the couch. She entered the only bedroom, ignored the lonely king-size bed staring back at her, and removed only her shoes and hose. She'd brought her sexiest pair of pajamas, which wasn't saying much. The soft jersey cotton felt great but didn't do much for sexy. But she needed to feel on an even keel with Noel. Something about him put her constantly off balance.

So she left on her dress, brushed out her hair, and joined him in the living area. He'd removed his jacket, socks and shoes, and rolled up his sleeves to his elbows. He had muscular forearms, she noted. Closer inspection showed a muscular build as well. Strange that he gave the appearance of being much smaller than he actually was.

"You ready?" He had a glass of what looked like alcohol by his side.

"I thought you didn't drink."

"Where did you get that idea?"

"You didn't order anything at dinner the other night."

"Ah. Well, I'm feeling mellow and secure in our suite. Would you like some?"

"What is it?"

"Scotch."

"Yech. No thanks."

"I also brought wine."

She thought about it. "Sure. Why not?" One glass of wine wouldn't turn her into a raving nympho. *Hell, I'm sober and already hot for his body.*

She didn't know why she kept giving herself a hard time for wanting the man. She had a normal attraction for a man she liked. Most of the time. When he wasn't being a pain or avoiding her.

"Here you go," he said, giving her a glass of red.

She sipped it and nodded. "This is good."

"Yes. I know."

She rolled her eyes. "Okay, Mr. Arrogant. Let's play."

She lost the first hand.

"My question." He sipped his Scotch and watched her with predatory intent. "Did I scare you after our date? Our coming together was pretty intense."

Trust him to go right for the kill. No "what's your favorite color?" from Noel.

"Um, well, I wasn't scared you'd hurt me or anything. But I wasn't prepared for that level of heat between us."

He nodded but didn't expand on his feelings. Of course not.

They played again, and she stopped at seventeen. Noel hit twenty and won.

"Next question. When's the last time you had sex before me?"

"Geez. A little personal, don't you think?"

He shrugged. "We got naked together. Not much more personal than that."

He had a point. "Well, hmm... More than a year ago. Two summers past, I think. I was dating a fellow teacher at the time. It didn't work out." She sighed and drank more wine. "What about you?"

He smirked. "I didn't lose. I don't have to answer you."

And so it continued, with her constantly fessing up while he interrogated her like a Spanish priest at the Inquisition. She finished her second glass of wine and realized she'd told him about her parents, her likes and dislikes, her friendship with Solene, dates with Brent and Mitch, and her student stories from this year. But not once did she learn anything new about him.

She felt warm but not tipsy or drunk, yet she shook her head when he asked if she wanted any more wine. "No, thanks. I need my head clear around you."

He smiled, and she saw the real Noel she'd started to fall for.

"You are either the luckiest man I know or you cheated. And don't give me that wounded look." Even his smirks turned her on. "Tell me something about you. Something personal that no one else knows."

His humor left him, and he stared at her with a somberness she found disconcerting. Being the center of all that focus was intense.

"I'm thinking of a career change." He seemed to surprise himself admitting that particular truth. "I'm tired, Addy. Tired of the travel and the hard work. It takes a toll."

She could only imagine.

"Hotels look the same after a while. The constant changes, the solitude, the moving around all the time. I want to put down roots."

"I get that. Trust me, I do." She was ready for a husband and children. But not yet, and not with Noel.

So why do I have to keep telling myself not to fantasize about happily ever after with him?

Because I'm a stupid romantic, that's why.

And because she'd never felt so deeply for a man, despite the fact that for the past two years she'd barely gotten a hello out of him.

"Do you?" he asked. "You have wonderful parents, a good life. Your students love you, your friends do too. You're a part of the community here, and you belong. I always feel like I'm passing through, never in one place long enough to really exist."

She put a hand over his, her smaller one covering his roughened exterior. "You think I don't understand, but I do. Yes, I belong in my community. But it can get lonely. I want to be special to one person. I want to love someone and have children, a house, pets. The whole works. I want warm holidays with children laughing and cooking for a rowdy bunch." She smiled. "It was just me and my parents growing up. Nana would come visit, or Aunt Tara, but for the most part we had a small family. And it was great. I wouldn't trade it for the world. But I miss being a part of that kind of belonging."

Remembering what he'd said about losing his parents, she squeezed his hand. "You'll have that someday too, Noel. But yeah, you probably do need to settle down to get it. It's got to be hard on relationships never being around."

He just stared at her, and she wondered what the heck he was thinking. He didn't look like he wanted to kiss her or sleep with her. He didn't look happy or sad, just very intent. On what?

Then he gave her a slow smile. "You're sneaky."

"What? Me?"

"You have a way of making me want to spill my guts. It's those soft green eyes, that gentle touch, that sincerity. I wish I had your skills."

"Gee, thanks, Noel." She dragged her hand out from under his. "I wasn't trying to trick you into sharing. I just wanted a little something, you know, since you pretty much got me to answer everything about me."

He gave her a sly grin. "I did, didn't I?"

Entranced by this playful side of him, she just nodded.

He leaned close and gave her a disappointing kiss on the cheek. "Well, it's late. I suppose we should turn in."

"Yes." She cleared her throat, determined to be in charge of herself tonight. No more succumbing to her libido. "Thanks for letting me have the bedroom."

He gave a mournful look at the couch and sighed. "No problem."

She refused to be the one to give in. He'd won everything else tonight. Not that she wanted to degrade their fledgling relationship to a game of one-upmanship, but Addy wanted to prove to herself she wasn't a needy, desperate woman. Plus, she didn't want the physicality between them to overshadow the emotional sharing they'd had tonight. She wanted to revel in how amazing it had felt to be on the arm of a man who treated her like she mattered.

As she retreated to the bedroom and readied for bed, she thought about Noel smiling and laughing. She'd seen him take in the show and genuinely like it. They had more in common than sexual chemistry. He was well-read and intelligent. Throughout their dinner, they'd verbally sparred, each making sound arguments on everything from politics to religion—two topics she normally strayed from when newly dating someone.

He held the same views she did, which surprised her, because she'd have pegged him as far more conservative. But Noel didn't hold bias against sexuality or gender. He didn't seem to care about playing games either. With Noel, it was all right or wrong, his morals not cloudy in the slightest. Heck, he believed in the death penalty. "Because some people just deserve to die," he'd said quietly.

Before she could follow that up, he'd tempted her into ordering dessert, and they'd said no more about grim subjects.

Addy slipped into bed and stilled, listening for Noel to fall asleep. He hadn't said anything about his accommodations for the night, but she hadn't seen a rollaway bed anywhere, and she didn't think the couch made out into a bed. Poor guy would have an uncomfortable night's sleep.

She wanted to feel badly about that but a grin curled her lips. *Ha. See? Just because I lost my mind once for you doesn't mean I can't control my urges.* She listened again but heard nothing from the living room.

Two hours later, she stared at the ceiling, her body on fire, her mind buzzing with thoughts of Noel and why he seemed so important lately. So vulnerable, when he always appeared in control of himself. So strong, able to stand against everyone.

"I always feel like I'm passing through, never in one place long enough to really exist," he'd said. Then she understood. His loneliness had drawn her to him from the beginning.

Having been an only child, she'd felt that same isolation. Oh, she knew love and acceptance from her parents, but when she'd left for college, then moved back only to find her parents moving out, she'd experienced that same sense of aloneness. Of not really belonging.

She taught other people's children. Dreamed of having a man of her own. Envied Solene's confidence and comfort around other people. Addy wouldn't call herself shy, exactly, but she didn't have that ease around people. Kids were easy to deal with. There was a pecking order, a need for discipline and balance. But adults made her uneasy, expectations always making her feel as if she lacked something.

Mitch had dumped her for another woman. That had hurt, but she hadn't loved him so the sting was mostly to her pride. Brent just didn't do it for her. Like most men she'd dated in her life, they didn't connect. She wished she could put her finger on it, but she couldn't explain why Noel felt so right when those others she'd spent months and even a year or more with never had.

Addy blew out a breath and wondered what the heck she was doing. She'd finally found a man she really liked. A man who might or might not be leaving again soon. He had issues. He was closed off. He might, in fact, have fathered a baby with a mysterious woman. And he still posed more questions than answers.

So what did she plan to do about him?

She finally had him all to herself. Why *shouldn't* she take what she wanted and see where the risks led her? Her father had known the moment he'd met her mother that she was the one for him. And he'd moved across the country to be with her. A huge risk.

Then again, Addy had friends on their third marriage, and that after having married and divorced their high school sweethearts. She sighed. What to do? Go big or go home? Did she risk her heart and take a chance on what might prove an amazing night, leading toward an amazing relationship? Or did she stay safe and be cautious? Remain the little school teacher who had nothing but her kids, her books, and a bitter best friend to keep her company?

Deciding to take charge of her life and embrace her strength as a sexual creature who could do whatever the hell she wanted, Addy quietly crept out of bed. She took a quick peek at herself in the bathroom and smoothed down her hair, wishing she looked sexier and less rumpled, then slid her door open and walked into the living room.

She stood over Noel, draped awkwardly on the couch, his feet hanging over the arm, his chest bared by the blanket tucked at his waist. From the moonlight illuminating the room in a faint glow, she saw his eyes closed. He looked perfect—handsome, muscular, at peace.

Then he opened his eyes, and she wondered if he'd been asleep at all.

His slow smile caused the heat inside her to unfurl. "What took you so long?"

NOEL HAD BEEN DYING INSIDE, minute by minute, waiting for Addy to figure out she needed him. As much as he needed her. It made little sense for a man born to caution, who worried about every last detail, to feel so much for a woman so soon. But in all fairness, he had been —not stalking—*investigating* her for years. He didn't deserve her. That sweetness, that inherent goodness Addy carried around so naturally.

But he craved it, craved *her*.

They had bantered at dinner, the conversation never stilted. And that was saying something for a man short on charm. Deacon or even Hammer could have flirted with her all night, seducing her out of her slinky dress. But Noel could only be himself, and he'd been able to relax into his own skin with her all night. That prickle of alarm when in public hadn't faded, but he'd thoroughly enjoyed her company.

And that affection made him desire her all the more. Her body had tantalized him all night. Every time she shifted and that dress teased at the supple flesh of her thighs. Or when she'd laugh and her hair had fluttered over her décolletage, hinting at the fullness of breasts he'd touched just a few days ago.

Fuck. He'd been aroused for hours, vacillating between lust and like as he considered all of Addy's attributes. A sharp woman who would only let him get away with so much, she'd managed to push past his barriers to get him to open up to her.

And that honesty compelled him to see the truth. The Business had worn thin years ago. Sure, Noel liked righting the world's wrongs, but death and destruction were eating at his soul. He couldn't brush off the kills anymore. He found himself thinking about that drugged-out girl in Bangkok. About the bastard children that Nigerian dictator had left behind after his death. About so much more than Noel could control.

Noel wanted his garden. He wanted his safe home with walls and doors that locked. He wanted Addy by his side. Her softness, her tenderness.

And in the deep secrets he didn't dare admit out loud, he wanted her love.

She stared down at him, and his heart filled, excitement and nerves jumbling while he waited for her to take that last step.

She frowned. "You knew I'd come?"

He shook his head, aware his erection made a tent in the

sheet. "I'd hoped. You have no idea how much I've hoped."

Her frown eased, and she glanced at the rising blanket with a slow smile. "That looks...uncomfortable."

"It really is."

She held her hand out to him. "Maybe you'd be better off in bed."

"Only if it's with you." He waited.

Her smile widened. "That's the plan."

He took her hand and shoved off the blanket. His boxer briefs did nothing to hide how much he wanted her.

She swallowed audibly. "You look good in underwear. Sorry my pajamas aren't that sexy."

He drew her to him and swore to himself when his arousal grew. *Slow down. Ease her into it.* "Trust me. I'm not seeing you in anything but skin. I have a great memory, and Tuesday night is burned into my brain."

Her sweet blush made him groan. He had to kiss her. The warmth of her mouth and the taste of minty toothpaste was so wholesome he had to smile.

"What's so funny?"

"I'm the luckiest guy in the world right now. And I'm not saying one more thing to chance it. Let's go." He pulled her with him toward the bedroom, then shimmied out of his underwear.

She stared at him, and he realized she hadn't seen him naked before.

"This is it, Addy. Oh, and one other thing." He left her and returned with a box of condoms. "I'm totally ready for you this time."

"Oh, right." She bit her lip and reached for the hem of her sleep shirt.

"Take it off," he said softly. "I want to see everything."

She tossed her shirt and pants to the floor, then slid her underwear down and stood straight and tall. Her nipples had beaded and her belly clenched, but she didn't cover herself at all.

After a moment, he admitted in a hoarse voice, "I'm not going to last the first time."

She blinked, then gave a shy smile.

He moved to the box and drew out a condom. She watched him like a hawk as he ripped the packet open then rolled it on. Fuck, just touching himself while she watched was enough to set him off, so he slowed down.

"Get on the bed and spread your legs," he ordered.

She laid back, still saying nothing.

"How kinky are you, Adeline Rose?" he asked her, crawling between her legs. Oh hell, she was wet and making no effort to hide it.

"How kinky?" she asked, her eyes shuttered, her lips parted. "I don't know."

"I'm going to fuck you tonight."

"I know."

"In your pussy." He watched her reaction to his plain talk and saw her blush, but he thought she liked it. "In your mouth." She licked her lips, and he groaned. "And in that tight ass." He stroked her thighs, still watching her expression. She didn't seem turned off or horrified by the idea. "You ever had anal, Addy?"

She gave a stiff nod. "Once, a few years ago. It was okay, but not great."

He smiled and leaned closer to her sweet sex. "Not then, not with the wrong man."

"Oh?" A challenge in her voice. The sexy school teacher was a go-getter in bed.

"Yeah. But with me, the *right* man, you'll be begging for me to finish you. And I'm going to drag it out."

"I thought you were afraid you wouldn't last?" she taunted.

"Not the first time. Not with such a feast in front of me." So saying, he shoved his face between her legs and went to work.

SEVEN

Addy couldn't believe it. None of this with Noel felt real, because just like the last time, she felt a dreamy lassitude cover her from head to toe. Nothing but carnal need turning her body into something foreign, unfamiliar.

Noel's body was covered in nothing but muscle...and some faint scars. He had many, but she couldn't dwell on them because the moment his hands touched her inner thighs, she was lost.

He stroked her and then his mouth was over her, sucking her clit between his lips and teeth. She jerked up, the pleasure too intense, but he clamped down on her thighs with those large, callused hands and kept her still. Controlling her, setting the pace, seducing her out of her mind.

She moaned his name, begging for more. Knowing she'd be the one to go off too soon, but unable to help it. Noel played her body so easily. How?

"Oh, yes, *yes*." She thrashed her head and clenched at his shoulders, needing more. Feeling so empty. "Please."

He moaned and sucked harder, then shoved his tongue inside her. But again, it wasn't enough, and she arched her hips to take more.

Noel squeezed her hips, then her ass, rubbing her cheeks then parting them, and she recalled he planned to take her in *every* way.

"Noel," she said panting. "I want you."

All she heard was a muffled acknowledgement while he continued to lick her, teasing with a mouth that should be outlawed. She'd never be able to watch him talk again, unable to stop imagining how he could melt her with that talented tongue.

She felt something probing her ass, and he slid his finger there while he shoved deeper into her pussy. She ground against him, needing some kind of penetration, even *back there*.

He pulled his mouth away to whisper, "Oh fuck, honey. Come over my tongue. I want you so bad." Then his mouth was back, wild and hungry as he sucked her clit with deep draws. The pressure at her ass retreated, and then his fingers stroked her labia before sliding deeper.

He eased one finger inside her, and she bucked, perilously close to orgasm.

The vibrated moan against her clit and addition of a second

finger inside her pushed her into a climax so intense she seized and kept on seizing, crying his name.

Then the fingers and mouth were gone and Noel was over her, in her, and plunging away while he kissed her.

She tasted herself on his tongue, felt his frantic need as he pounded inside. She gripped him while she continued to come, undone by this ungodly orgasm.

Noel swore and shoved so hard the bed shook. He stayed there, over her, and pumped as he came.

She stroked his ribs and back as she came down off the same high, boneless and so satisfied she wanted to sleep forever in his arms.

"Damn, Addy." He whispered her name again, then leaned down to kiss her, all while remaining inside her.

She blinked her eyes open, not sure when she'd closed them. His dark brown eyes shimmered with pleasure, his lips parted while he caught his breath. But his body remained hard, strong.

She stroked his shoulders. "You're so much bigger than I thought you were."

He raised a brow.

She flushed. "I meant your arms and chest. Not that." She contracted her inner muscles, and he gasped. "That's as big as I imagined." She chuckled.

"Damn. You kill me. Wait, stop laughing." He withdrew,

disposed of the condom, and remained on top of her. "Sorry about that. That was only round one. We'll go slower next time." His satisfied grin did something to her, made her fall hard and fast with no reason why. Just seeing him happy, unguarded, caused her need for him to flare.

"Next time? I don't think I can move."

He cradled her to him then rolled over, so she lay on his stomach. "Nah. You're a lot stronger than you look."

"Thanks a lot," she grumbled, pleased to see him playing with her.

The sparkle in his eyes mesmerized, so she let him do whatever he wanted. He continued to pet her, learning all her curves and lines. He sat her up over him, and she was surprised to feel him firming under her. Didn't most men need time to get back their game?

"Are you getting hard?"

"I stay hard, honey. You have me sated, but not all the way. Not yet. But I don't need to be hard to be happy." He ran his hands up her thighs, on either side of him, to her waist and belly. He traced her stomach and raised his fingers along her ribs. "You are so sexy. I want to lick you up all over again."

Her cheeks felt hot. She was still wet and sliding over his cock. "That was really good."

"Yeah, it was." He cupped her breasts, and she hissed her

pleasure. "But these. I've neglected these pretty little nipples."

He drew her down to him and took one breast in his mouth.

She started, but he held her down with a hand on her waist, the other cupped around her breast.

He sucked her nipple deep, then bit lightly and caused new heat to flare between her legs. "Yeah, you like that." He glanced at her before turning his attention to her other breast. "God, I love your body. You always get me so hard." He groaned and sucked her, lingering over the tips before shoving her breasts together, so he could suck one then the other. "What do you want next, honey?"

"Wh-what?" She couldn't help grinding over him, feeling him rock hard and hot under her.

"Your ass or your mouth?" he whispered against her breasts.

Addy wanted it all, still stunned to know that her body could reach such heights. "You pick."

"Fuck." He leaned back and lifted her up, then settled her back over him. This time he angled himself so that she slid down his shaft, taking him inside.

"Noel," she moaned.

"I know. Baby, I know." He raised her up and down over him, his grip tight, his control a thing of beauty. "Damn. You feel so fucking good." He arched up into her, faster, harder, then stopped suddenly. "Wait." He closed his eyes and held her still.

She knew chancing it once without a condom had been risky. But she wanted to see him lose control. To spill inside her and give her that pleasure all over again, knowing she had all of him.

But Noel lifted her off and rolled to his knees. He sat with his back against the headboard and motioned her closer. "Come on, Addy. Let's see that pretty mouth around my cock."

Tingling with the thrill of doing something so naughty, so sexy, she did the crawling this time and rested between his legs on her hands and knees.

Noel stared with bright eyes, fixated on her hanging breasts. "You have no idea how many times I imagined this."

That surprised her. "What?"

He moaned and cupped his erection. "Oh yeah. I used to come home and see my perky, sexy neighbor. And it was all I could do to get away from you before I jumped you."

"Really?" Such a sweet thing to say. Kind of. She contained an overjoyed laugh. He'd wanted to *jump* her.

"Yeah, Addy. I wanted you all the time. But I'm not a nice guy. I'm not good enough for you." He looked her in the eye, his expression mean, possessive. "But I don't care anymore. I want you. You're mine."

For how long? No. tonight wasn't for planning futures. It was for living out a fantasy. For feeling good and not worrying about tomorrow. "That's right," she agreed. "As much as you're mine." She leaned down, closer to that thick flesh swelling for her.

Then she removed his hand so she could wrap hers around the base.

He moaned and tensed all over. A very good sign.

She took a mental picture. Noel, aroused, reminded her of a hungry panther. All dark lines and edges. She licked his cockhead, lapping at the fluid there, and he clenched her shoulder, then eased his fingers.

"Addy... I'm clean. God, I want you to swallow me down. All of it. But you don't have to. You—" He bit off his next words when she eased her mouth down him, taking in the thick cockhead and going farther. But she had to stop midway, because he was too big. She angled herself, putting her ass in the air while her head bobbed over him, getting accustomed to his size.

He cradled her cheek and held tight to her shoulder while she took him, and all the while he jerked in her mouth, his need growing.

"Shit, Addy. I'm so close..."

She cupped his sac and rubbed while taking him deeper, almost to the back of her throat. She gagged once but didn't stop.

And then Noel was moving with her, pushing for her to take more.

"Please, baby. Please," he begged while she regrouped and took him past her reflex into a spot that worked. "Now, yes, Oh God. *Now,*" he said between grunts and released down her throat while she swallowed.

She eased back after a moment and gave a few more sucks before he stopped her and finished coming. She'd swallowed a lot from a man who'd just climaxed not long before, and she liked that he had stamina.

Addy knelt in front of him, pleased to see him so wrung out.

He blinked at her. "Holy shit."

She smiled.

"You are one deadly woman."

"Deadly. Not sure if I like that description."

Noel weakly put a hand over hers. "Trust me. It's a compliment."

She laughed. "I think I tired you out."

"Damn. You might have. But I won't leave you high and dry." He had a gleam in his eyes she didn't trust.

And she shouldn't have. Because he had her on her back, his hands and mouth everywhere. And then he showed her that his fingers could work the same magic as his mouth as he brought her to a quick yet earth-shattering orgasm.

When she could breathe again, she found him looking down at her, a man well satisfied. "So we've hit two out of three." He smiled wide. "Don't worry, honey. I'm going to tap that fine ass soon enough. How about we clean up and get some rest first?"

She nodded, done in, and let him tend to her.

Then she slept in his arms, and the feeling of warmth and comfort turned their sexy night into something a lot deeper.

WHEN ADDY WOKE the next morning, Noel tightened his arm around her waist. "I need the bathroom," she whispered, and he immediately let go and turned onto his back, still sleeping.

Addy used the facilities then checked the time. Seven in the morning. She wanted to do something nice for Noel. Last night had been more than she could have imagined. Somehow lust had turned into what felt like love. Crazy and overemotional. She'd make sure to talk herself off the ledge as soon as their mini-vacation ended. Later today.

For now she'd bask in the feeling. She tiptoed back into the room, quickly threw her clothes on, and stared at him. Even asleep he looked hard, unrelenting.

Her entire body quivered, and she smiled. She walked over to him and planted a kiss on his cheek. To her surprise, he wrapped an arm around her and tugged her into bed, where he gave her a thorough kiss.

"Wow," she said when he eased up. "Not even a bad case of morning breath. That was great."

He gave a gravelly chuckle. "I popped a mint while you were in the bathroom."

"Cheater."

"You'd rather I hit you with my dragon breath?"

Addy scrunched her nose. "Ew. Good point." She scrambled off the bed and saw him lying there, lounging like a giant cat pretending to be tame. She swallowed a lovesick sigh. "Because you've been so nice to me, I'm going to get us a treat. Don't move. I'll be right back!"

"Wait. Addy—"

She grabbed the keycard off the counter, as well as her purse. Speeding out before he got up and wasn't so naked anymore, she texted him from the elevator to relax and wait for her. In the lobby she asked the concierge about the best place to get something for breakfast.

Heading for Morning Josefine, an amazing patisserie, she hurried in the brisk fall morning air but fortunately only had to wait in a short line.

After purchasing two coffees and a bag of goodies, she walked back the way she'd come. An incoming alert on her phone had her pausing to read a text from…Deacon?

Odd. She read the message, asking her to meet him in a store that happened to be a few doors down. An emergency, he'd said, so she'd save her questions as to how he'd known where they were staying until she saw him. Hopefully the baby was okay. She fumbled with the bag and coffee but managed to text him back. Then she turned and sought out a storefront with the black and gold sign on the front.

She found it over what looked like an abandoned storefront, one that had gone out of business. The blinds were all closed, hiding the store from sight. Even the front door had a length of curtain hiding the interior. She put the coffee holder down on the ground and knocked at the door.

"Deacon?" She turned the knob, not expecting it to be open, and it turned. She grabbed her coffee and walked inside.

The place had been a restaurant or deli of some kind, because there were still tables and stools and counters in place, though dust covered the surfaces. She set down her stuff and shut the door after her.

But the interior looked too dark, with only slivers of morning light filtering in from the front blinds. "Deacon?" she called again, then turned to open a set of blinds so she could see.

Hands grabbed her and startled her into a yelp. "Not yet, sweetheart." She didn't recognize the voice or the rough grip. Fear overwhelmed her, and she struggled to get free. But her captor seemed so much bigger and stronger. Panicked, she tried to turn to see him. "I'm gonna break your sexy little neck, bitch. And won't that make him so sad?"

Then all hell broke loose. What sounded like muffled pops, stools breaking, and swearing added to the scent of blood, suddenly pooling beneath her feet.

She shrieked and jerked out of her assailant's arms—right into Noel.

"Are you okay?" he growled. "Addy, are you okay?"

She nodded, shaky and confused.

He pushed her toward the front door and tucked her under a counter. "Stay low and don't leave."

She nodded, still unsure what the hell was going on.

The door had closed again, and Noel was fighting with someone. But on the floor in front of her lay a man with his eyes closed, a bullet lodged in the center of his forehead.

None of it looked real. It couldn't be real, could it? This had to be some kind of gag. Where was Deacon?

Noel and the tall man he fought returned to view, and she watched in astonishment as Noel used hand-to-hand moves she'd once seen in a Kung Fu movie. He moved with grace and lethal purpose as he smacked a knife out of the tall man's hands, then struck his forearm at the man's throat, kicked at his knee, and aimed another blow at his solar plexus. He then flipped the man onto his back, the guy landing in the blood next to his associate.

A gun appeared in Noel's hand, and he shoved it under his enemy's chin. In a calm voice that scared the crap out of her because it was so unemotional, he said, "Who sent you?"

"Fuck you," the guy wheezed.

Addy wondered if he'd broken some ribs, because the man sounded in pain and was having a difficult time breathing.

Noel stared, his gaze emptier than anything she'd seen. Then he removed the gun from the underside of the man's chin and shot him in the knee. The man would have screamed loud enough to bring attention had Noel not covered his mouth. Noel returned the gun to the man's throat. "Your name, or you lose the other knee."

It was like something out of a gangster movie. *Oh my God. Noel shot someone.* She glanced at the dead body. *Killed someone.*

"I can get it off your prints easily enough," Noel said quietly. "But I'll let you live if you give it to me."

Her mouth dry, Addy found it hard to breathe.

"Wilkes, you bastard. Yeah, you know that name. You killed my brother."

What?

Noel aimed the gun higher, at the man's thigh. "Femoral arteries can be tricky things. Who's your friend?" He nodded to the dead man.

"I just met Rene yesterday. And before you ask again, I

can't tell you who hired me. It was a contract hit. You know how that works."

Noel shot a glance at Addy, then murmured something to the guy she couldn't make out. He pulled back the gun, then slammed it into the man's head and knocked him out. Then Noel was on his phone, asking someone named Big Joe for assistance.

He hung up, stood, then found tape to tie up the living guy's hands. The dead body he left bleeding all over the floor. Noel moved to the front door and locked it. Then he crouched by Addy, who couldn't stop shivering.

He sighed and held out a hand. "It's okay, honey. The danger's gone."

When she just stared at him, fuzzy and weepy and scared, he stroked her cheek. And he looked...sad.

"I'm so sorry, Addy. If I'd thought you could be in danger, I never would have brought you with me." Then he tugged her to her feet and shocked her once more. He hugged her tight, patted her back, and she let the tears fall.

NOEL FELT LIKE ABSOLUTE SHIT. Had he been just a few minutes faster, it wouldn't have taken him so long to track her down. As it was, he'd almost had a heart attack when he'd burst into the abandoned storefront to see some dickhead with a gun in one hand grabbing her by the throat.

To be honest, he'd expected more of a fight. But Rene had gone down too easily. Wilkes had challenged him, but with nothing Noel couldn't handle. Again, these assailants just didn't measure up. No way the Business had sent them.

So where did that leave him?

With a frightened woman he'd just exposed to intense violence. A woman who would never look at him the same way again. He hugged her tighter and turned her from the bodies. Poor Addy. She should never have borne witness to this.

"We should call 911," she whispered.

"We can't. I'll explain soon. Come on, Addy. Let's go." He stepped her around the guys, knowing Big Joe's team would sweep the mess under the rug and look into Wilkes and his story. Leaving him alive grated, but Noel hadn't wanted to kill anyone else in front of Addy. Not if he didn't need to.

He walked her out the back, tucking his pistol in the back of his jeans and covering up with his coat.

She said something, still leaning against his chest, clinging to him like a burr.

"What's that?" He felt an urge to protect, to keep her safe, that went deeper than any need for justice or anger. Concern for Addy was his top priority.

"The c-coffee and p-past-tries are b-back there." She sobbed as she added, "I g-got them for y-you."

God. What a mess. He kissed the top of her head and pulled them into a shadowed alley between two shops. "Addy, I'm so sorry. So very sorry. It's okay. You're safe. I'll never let anything happen to you."

She wiped her eyes on his sweater and pulled back. But even crying, she was the most beautiful thing he'd ever seen. "What happened, Noel? W-why did you have a gun? Why no police?"

"I'll tell you back at the hotel, okay?"

"I want coffee. R-right now."

She didn't seem too together, her eyes still glassy, her voice shaky. But he would do anything to make her feel better.

"Okay."

"From...Morning Josefine."

He'd passed it on his way to rescue her, almost too late as he'd seen her disappear inside the old diner. "If that's what you want." He wiped her eyes. "Don't cry, honey. I swear, I'll explain all this." And if she never wanted to see him again, he'd leave. It would kill him, but he'd leave.

Content that no one would move on her in so crowded a spot, he sat her at a corner table in the busy cafe, where he could see her while he stood in line to get her coffee. He fetched them two coffees and a bundle of sweets, then returned to her.

"Let's go."

"No." She frowned. "I want to stay here."

He sighed. "Fine." He pushed her coffee near her.

She sipped it and looked at him in surprise. "This is good. Just the way I take it."

Of course it was. Noel knew a lot about her. "I pay attention."

"I guess you do." She tentatively looked in the bag but didn't reach for any food. "Noel. Talk."

He sipped his coffee, considering how much to tell her. "I'm not actually an investment banker."

She narrowed her eyes but said nothing.

In a low voice, he said, "I work for an organization that cleans up messes around the world."

She put her coffee down. "What organization?"

"I can't say."

"Can't or won't?" she challenged in a louder voice. Then seeing his frown, she lowered hers again. "CIA? FBI? NSA?"

He nodded.

She blinked and trembled. "Seriously?"

"I'm not on any books. Not in any database. I don't exist, Addy. But I want to." So much. He hadn't been lying when he'd told her that last night. He glanced around, saw them still somewhat safe surrounded by couples and young mothers and fathers with kids. "I was young when my parents died. I had no one to take me in. I tried foster care. It didn't take." He didn't want her to feel sorry for him, but better pity than fear. "I was on the streets for a very long year when a man found me. He introduced me to a new career path."

"How old were you?" She sipped her coffee, and her shaking finally subsided.

"Fourteen. They taught me a lot." He remembered the days of brutal drills, of shooting on the line, of martial arts training. The nonstop learning, studying languages, political machinations, history, and tactics. No weekends or summers off. But he'd belonged, as he hadn't in a long time. "I went out solo at eighteen and never stopped."

She sat there for some time, then asked, "Deacon and Hammer?"

"Just like me."

She nodded before a hurt look appeared on her face. "So it was all lies?" She paused. "What about Noel Jr.?"

He grimaced. "He's real. The mess I'm in with him is real. My home in Bainbridge, being with you, all real." He took her hand, pleased she didn't pull away, but not happy she stiffened under him. "I wasn't lying about the rest either. I need a change."

She snorted, surprising him with that hint of sass. "I'd say you do if your workdays are like what you just did."

He nodded. "More or less. I get by telling myself it's for the greater good. One less dictator who kills the masses. One less drug runner selling young girls and boys in trade. One less corrupt official contributing to mass murder in war-torn countries. But Addy, that kind of work leaves a stain. And I'm tired."

She looked at him, really looked at him, and he wondered what she saw. Then she glanced away and stood. "I want to go home, Noel."

So he took her. But the quiet ride on the ferry had never felt so long.

EIGHT

Addy hugged herself as she sat in Noel's car while he stood outside, leaning against the driver's side door. Despite all that had happened, she wasn't afraid of him.

The minute they'd boarded the ferry, she'd taken a trip to the bathroom and sidelined to a payphone, where she'd dialed the police to give an anonymous report of trouble at the abandoned storefront. Five minutes ago she'd gone to "use the restroom" again and called back, only to find out the police had found nothing in that store. No bodies. No blood. Nothing broken or cracked in the shop at all and could she please leave her name because it was a crime to falsify a 911 call.

She had to be crazy to believe Noel's story. A spy? She wasn't born yesterday. But who had cleaned up after him? And if he wasn't what he said he was, who was he? A killer for hire? She'd watched him shoot a man in cold blood. Granted, that man had tried to hurt her for some reason, but Noel hadn't killed the second man. Instead, he'd called in help.

Could he really have been trained to be a killer? Deacon or Hammer she could see in that type of profession. But quiet, steady, hermit-like Noel? Though, that would explain the scars on his body. And the lost look in his eyes.

And she still didn't fear him. Instead, she felt bad for him, because she *did* believe him. So much of what he'd told her made sense about the man she now knew.

No family, only violence to bring him to adulthood. All his talk about the greater good. She'd grown up hearing about her father working for the greater good. Bert Rose had retired after thirty years on the police force. Addy knew all about helping others, about service to one's country, city, people.

She'd thought she'd known Noel, and she'd been wrong. Addy had assumed she could read people.

She glanced out the car window and saw him with his arms wrapped around himself, no doubt cold because of the winds off the Sound. But he wouldn't go upstairs inside the ferry and leave her alone down by the cars, away from the safety of others. She could tell her having been in danger bothered him.

Unless it was all an act?

No. He'd been genuinely upset that she'd been harmed. His quick actions had saved her. Noel could have dumped her. Could have run away and left her to fend for herself.

Hell, he'd even sat with her at a public coffee shop, risking that she'd call the authorities and report him. She still had her cell phone.

But she'd called to report the incident, not Noel. And why not?

Because he hadn't ditched or kidnapped her. Instead, he'd called Deacon and Hammer to tell them what had happened. Then he'd given her some long looks, and a few dejected ones when he hadn't thought she'd been watching. He was taking her home, as she'd asked.

And he'd mentioned something to Hammer about packing up and leaving.

That wouldn't do.

She knocked on the driver's side window.

He leaned down, and she motioned to him to come back inside.

He entered and shut the door behind him. The car felt a lot smaller all of a sudden.

"One thing I still don't understand," she said. "Deacon texted me to meet him."

Noel shook his head. "It wasn't Deacon. He's spent the past few days on the island arguing with Solene about childcare, apparently. And he spent last night in Canada, sent on a wild goose chase while Hammer wrapped things up out East. Both of them should be back soon, though."

"Good."

"Addy, I'm sorry."

"So you keep saying." She'd gotten her courage back, and it felt good. Seeing a man get killed was nothing like the movies. The finality of that moment would be forever etched in her mind. But she could deal better, now.

"I never wanted that world to intrude on this one." He clenched his hands around the steering wheel. "When I come back from a job, I meditate on the ferry ride. Do you ever do that?"

"No."

"I put all the ugliness that's in the world behind me. I look forward to feeling fresh. I'm normal here. Just a guy settling into his house. Fixing the plumbing. Checking out my cute neighbor when she's not looking." He sent her a ghost of a smile that faded too soon. "Keeping to myself, because I know life in Bainbridge Island isn't real. Not for me."

For someone so young, he must have seen a lot of nasty things.

"Noel."

"I don't want you to feel sorry for me, Addy. I live the life, and someday all that violence is going to find me. No matter how careful I've been, it's followed me here. I've had my handler looking into it for me. And Deacon and Hammer too.

"The baby was a complete surprise. Look, I'm not a monk. But it takes a lot for me to let down my guard with a person."

Yet he'd done it with her.

"Having sex is getting vulnerable. So I don't do it a lot. And I'm always—usually—careful. The baby isn't mine. I just know it. But if he were, I'd take care of him. I might be a killer, but I'm a protector at heart. No boy of mine would ever want for security."

She believed him.

"Thing is, something went wrong after my last job. Not on the job exactly, but on my return home. I was nearly mugged in the city. Then I was almost run down on the street. Then this, today. None of it makes any sense. We're a closely guarded secret, Addy. No one but my handler and his boss know my missions. I said I work for the government, but my Business contracts out the jobs. Seriously. I don't exist. Noel Cavanaugh works for an investment firm. He's good at what he does. But he's not me."

She thought about that. "Is Noel Cavanaugh even your real name?"

He watched her, and she swore he looked for a brief second as if he still had hope—for her? "Noel is real. Cavanaugh isn't though." He paused. "My last name is Smith, believe it or not. Noel Smith."

"Really?" She smiled, seeing the humor in such a common name for an uncommon man. She took his hand in hers, feeling for him when he gripped her tight. "Noel, why did you ask me out?"

He flushed but didn't look away. "I wanted to go out with you."

"For two years you've ignored or avoided me. Why now?"

He sighed. "I don't know. If I'd been smart, I would have stayed away. Addy, I've known about you for a long time, even before you moved back. I'm a cautious guy. I have to be. I researched all my neighbors. My closest ones especially." He rubbed a thumb over her hand. "When you moved back to Bainbridge, it was so hard to stay away. I liked you from the start. But I didn't want to drag you down. I'm not a safe man. I'm not a nine-to-fiver working for stock options with dinner and a movie on the brain."

"So you just wanted in my pants, is that it?"

He scowled. "Hell no. I mean, yeah, I wanted to have sex with you. You're beautiful, smart, funny. Why wouldn't I? But you're sweet, nice. Damn, Addy, you teach school kids. I *kill* people for a living. It's not a good mix."

"But…?"

"But then you handed me a baby on my doorstep. He made me see that my wanting to get out of the job has been building. I've been contracting for twelve years. I'm only thirty, and I'm burned out."

"I sense that." She held him. "Do you really like gardening?"

He gave her a small grin that tugged at her heartstrings. "I really do. I wasn't lying about all of it, like I said. I'm actually very boring. I don't like going out. I'm a homebody. When I'm home, where it's safe, I garden. I read. I try to pretend I don't want you," he said wryly before pulling his hand away. "Watching a sunset, hearing the birds and watching them fly overhead, that's magic to me. But it was nothing compared to last night." He swallowed, his heart in his eyes. "Last night meant something to me."

"It meant something to me too." What, was the question. "Okay. So let's say I trust what you've told me. Where do we go from here?"

"*I* go far away," he said firmly. "Away from you, so the danger's gone. Then I finish figuring out who's behind this."

"No."

"I—what?" He frowned.

"They came for me once. What's to say they won't do it again?"

He gritted his teeth.

"I'm safer with you than without you."

"Addy, I won't put you in danger again."

"You will if you leave me alone."

"I—crap." He leaned his head back and closed his eyes. "You don't understand. I can't let them hurt you."

"So don't. Get Deacon and Hammer back here and figure out what's going on. And figure out what to do about Noel Jr."

He blew out a breath. "Easier said than done." He turned to look at her. "You're really okay with all I said? With everything that happened?"

"No, but I'm adaptable. You know my dad was a cop?"

"Yeah. And a helluva gardener."

"He still *is* a helluva gardener. He's just growing crops in Scotland now." She scooted closer to him in the car. "Noel, I won't lie. I'm scared. But I don't want you to leave, not now." She clutched him by the arm. "You said last night meant something to you."

"It did."

"Then stick around and find out what."

He looked down at her. "You sure, Addy? I'm all into seeing where this goes if you are. But if anything ever happened to you…" He stroked her cheek. "I'd send them all to hell. It would be a bloodbath. No one gets to you unless they go through me first."

Her quiet Noel, ferocious when it counted. "You don't scare me, Noel Smith. Not unless you plan on leaving without saying goodbye." Hell, if he planned on leaving period. But Noel was understandably skittish. She decided to keep him around, so she'd have to move slowly, so as not to spook him.

Like dealing with a small child, she'd win him over with patience and trust. And since he certainly *wasn't* a small child, she'd know exactly how to handle him. She smiled at him, and he did a double take before starting the car and getting ready to depart the ferry as they pulled into Bainbridge Island.

"We can do this, Noel. Together."

"I'm willing to try. But Addy, like I said, I won't—*can't*—let you get hurt because of me. If it comes down to that, I'll leave."

"Okay, Noel."

Bullshit. I'm not letting you go yet. Not now. Maybe not ever.

NOEL STILL WASN'T sure how she'd talked him into staying in town. But hell, she hadn't bolted yet, so he had hope she might give him another chance. That Addy could handle him killing a man in front of her and not run away screaming said a lot for her strength of will, her courage.

He drove them both toward his house when something Deacon had said struck him. He pulled over to the side of the road and dialed Deacon on speaker. "Deacon? Where's the baby?"

Addy shot him a worried look.

"I told you," Deacon drawled.

"You told me you had to check something out in Canada, so I assumed you'd taken care of babysitting for the kid. Did you take him with you?"

"I left Noel Jr. with Solene. She wasn't happy about it, but I paid her triple her usual rate. The shark." He muttered something else.

"What?"

"Not important. I'll be home tomorrow afternoon. And buddy, you owe me big for all that babysitting I'm doing."

"You mean watching your own kid, don't you? Isn't he saying your name now?"

"He shit all over my favorite pants!"

Noel couldn't hide a grin. "Sorry, you're breaking up." Even Addy smiled.

"Noel, you bastard, don't even think about—"

Noel disconnected and turned to Addy. "So the baby is with Solene. I think we'd better go get him."

"Yeah. Especially because Solene isn't a babysitter. She runs a daycare, but when she goes home for the night, she's baby-less. I'm dying to know how Deacon convinced her to watch Noel Jr."

He sighed. "That's not his name."

"I think it's cute."

"I think the kid deserves something a little more creative than Noel Jr."

They argued about names on the short drive to Solene's home, just like a normal couple. Noel prayed that ease between them would continue.

Solene lived in a gorgeous, semi-private home in Manitou Beach, just four and a half miles from Addy.

"Nice place," Noel said as they left the car.

Solene opened the front door before they reached it. "Noel Jr. is napping. And Noel, you owe me big time."

Addy grinned. "You sound just like Deacon."

Frost glazed Solene's amber eyes. "*Don't* mention that man's name to me, Addy. Not if you want to stay friends."

Noel sighed. "What did he do?"

"When he wasn't flirting with me or my staff, you mean? Or the mothers dropping their kids off? Or the women working next door at the friggin' bakery? He had the nerve to try to bully me into helping him. When that didn't work, he manipulated me into caring for Noel Jr.!"

Noel kept his face expressionless, certain he'd get smacked if he showed any sign of amusement. "Manipulated how?"

"He said he was going into danger. That the baby might get hurt if he had to take him, and he didn't want to chance it." She huffed. "How could I let that precious baby get hurt if I could stop it? That rat bastard," she seethed.

"I assume you mean Deacon and not the baby."

Solene gave him a baleful eye. "Of course I'm not referring to the baby. You might be cute, but you're a little short on smarts, eh?" She turned. "Well, come on, you two. Tell me how the date went."

Noel and Addy exchanged a glance before following Solene inside.

The open floor plan had dark hardwoods throughout, and the airy rooms were breathtaking, but not as awe-inspiring as the view out the bay windows at the back of the house, overlooking the water.

"Yeah, yeah, you can see the water and Seattle from here." She gathered up a familiar duffle bag and plopped it at Noel's feet. Then she left and returned carrying a sleeping baby in his baby carrier. She put him down and added quietly, "Well? The date?"

Noel knew he'd need to let Solene know about the possible danger, especially since she'd be linked to him sooner or later because of the baby and Addy.

"It was...interesting," Addy answered. "Noel, why don't I stay with Solene while you get little Griffith settled?"

He rolled his eyes, secretly thrilled she still was teasing him. "Griffith? Really? Why don't you paint a sign on his back begging kids to beat him up on the playground too?"

Solene looked confused. "I thought his name was Noel Jr.?"

"No, that's just what Deacon calls him to annoy me."

"Yeah, about that. So who is the baby's father, anyway? Because I am seriously baffled about all of this."

"I'll explain things," Addy said. "Then you can drive me back to Noel's after I get settled for a bit."

Noel sighed. "Probably a good idea. I'll take little Gunnar home with me. Come on, fella. Let's go." He glanced down at the sleeping bundle. "I really like him like this."

Solene smothered a chuckle. "Hold on and I'll get you his car seat."

Once she'd put it in the back seat, he locked the baby carrier in and made sure the boy was secure, then turned to Solene. "Thanks for this. I know Deacon bullied you into it, but you really did a good thing. Deacon wasn't lying about things not being so safe."

"What?"

"Addy will explain. And Solene, be her friend. She needs you right now."

Solene just watched him. A gorgeous woman with light brown eyes, golden wavy hair, and the feminine features of an angel and seductress both, she was more than striking. Her body was lean and curvy in all the right ways, her voice husky, stroking along sensual centers in the brain.

Yet he didn't desire her at all. He had eyes only for Addy, with her almond-shaped eyes, her creamy skin, and shiny black hair, so straight and soft he wanted to pet her every time he saw her. Her body knocked him for a loop, but it was Addy's vibrant warmth that had him wanting to be near her more and more. And to see her react so well under such horrific conditions. A man couldn't ask for a better woman by his side.

He waved to Solene, got in, and started up the car. "Just you and me, kid," he said to the boy and drove back home.

What, exactly, would Addy tell Solene? He hadn't told her to keep anything a secret, though he should have. Yet he trusted her judgment. Aside from the mess their date had become, he hoped she remembered their time together before all the violence. She'd said it meant something to her, and hopefully she wouldn't find it so easy to forget.

God help him, he sure couldn't.

SOLENE WENT BACK INSIDE, puzzled and pleased at the same time.

"Thanks for watching the baby," Addy said. She looked tired and a little off balance.

"What happened with you two?"

Something big, because Solene could all but see the confusion stamped on her friend's face. She loved Addy, but her friend had the tendency to overthink things. Noel, the man who rarely smiled or laughed, had rolled his eyes at her friend. He'd been caring, attentive, and from all Addy had said, he never acted that way.

"Addy," she prodded. "Tell me."

She wasn't prepared for her friend to burst into tears.

"Oh sweetie. Are you okay?" She hurried to get Addy seated with her on the couch and hugged her. Then she drew a box of tissues close and handed her one.

Addy blew her nose.

"Did he hurt you? Was he out of line?" Her imagination worked overtime. "Do you want me to call the police?"

"*No.* No police." Addy started laughing, a little bit of hysteria, Solene thought. "You would not believe my day."

"Start at the beginning."

Addy groaned. "I was crazy to go out with him. We both know he's not the stick-around kind of guy. But I've had this, I don't know, crush on him for years. Our date was awesome. We had dinner, saw a play... It was weird how well we got along. We like a lot of the same things, and he's fun to debate with."

Solene kept quiet, hearing the joy in Addy's words. So she wouldn't go over to Noel's house and clobber him—yet.

"Then we went back to the hotel. It was beautiful, romantic. And we played cards."

Solene frowned. "Cards?"

"Yes. See, the first time we were together—"

"Had sex, you mean."

Addy huffed. "Had sex, it was so out of control and wild, neither of us were prepared. It hit Noel as hard as it hit me. So this time he rented a suite and I got the bedroom. He said he'd leave it up to me whether or not we had sex, since I was obviously ga-ga for him."

"He said that?"

"Not in so many words, but that's what he meant." Addy paused. "And I am ga-ga for him, which makes this so much worse. I'm the one who initiated sex. The night was *so much* better than anything I could have imagined." Addy sighed. "He was so amazing, and he made me feel so good. Not just physically either. He was tender and caring and…" She tapered off into a sniffle. "So this morning I wanted to do something nice for him. I went out to get us some pastries and coffee. Then Deacon texted me."

Solene stiffened. "Deacon?" That creep! Making moves on Addy right after she'd been with his friend? And after flirting with *her*?

"He said something about an emergency with the baby. So I met him at this empty restaurant and was attacked." She swallowed. "But not by Deacon."

"Oh no." Solene put a hand on Addy's knee. "What happened?"

"It was all so fast. This stranger put his hands around my

throat and threatened to kill me. Then Noel was there. He —" Addy took a deep breath and whispered "—he *killed* a man, Solene. And he hurt the other man with him. Then we left."

"You just left?" This sounded crazy. "I'm calling the police."

"No." Addy grabbed her hand. "You can't." She drew in a breath and let it out. "Noel isn't an investment banker. He works for the government. He called someone to clean up after we left. Solene, *I* called the police after it happened, and they said there was nothing there. His people made it disappear. Who does that?"

"Holy shit. So is he a spy or something?" Solene looked around her, wondering if even now she was being monitored. She had to stop watching all those crime shows. But seriously. Noel? A spy?

"Not a spy. He said he takes care of problems around the world. I think... I think he's someone who gets rid of the bad guys. Permanently."

"Like a hitman or something? An assassin?" Noel, a killer? Was she wrong for being fascinated instead of scared out of her mind? Okay, so a little part of her was freaked out. But...*Noel*? A man who ironed his freakin' jeans?

"I didn't say hitman."

"No, but we're both thinking it. Wow. Just...wow." A thought struck her. "Deacon? Is he one too?"

"I kind of think yes. Noel said he and the others don't exist in any database or anything. No way to back up what he's saying as true, but I saw him in action. He's deadly."

Now anxiety reared its head. "Should we leave? Get you out of town? I have money. I could make it happen."

"I'm not afraid of him." Addy shook her head, her green eyes dark. "I should be, but I'm not. He'd never hurt me, Solene."

"How do you know that? You barely know the guy."

"I know enough. He wants to leave the business, to come here and just be Noel Cavanaugh. Especially now with the baby."

"Yeah, the baby." Solene didn't understand any of this. "Is the boy his or some kind of cover story?"

"The baby is another part of the mystery around Noel. Someone is trying to kill him, and someone dropped off the baby saying it's either his, Deacon's, or Hammer's."

Solene's heart raced. "Seriously?"

"Yes. I know I should stay out of his mess, but now I'm in it. They tried to kill me to get to him."

"Shit. This isn't good at all, Addy."

"I know. But I still want to be with him. Am I crazy or what?" Addy gave a half laugh, half sob. "He's the one for me, Solene. It's weird and nutty and I don't care. I connect with him on a level I've never had with anyone else. And it just figures he's a killer for hire."

"That's some weird-ass karma for sure," Solene teased, half out of her mind with concern. "Do I need to worry that he'll kill *me* if he knows I know about him?"

"No." Good. At least Addy sounded definite about that. "He's a good man. And right now I think he needs me."

"Right now? What about later?"

"I hope he meant it when he said Friday night was special to him. Because I think I'm falling in love with him."

"Falling? You mean fall-*en*, right? Past tense. You're the teacher and all, but I'd say you're gone for the guy."

"Crap. I am."

They sat in silence for a moment. "Okay," Solene said. "This is what we're going to do. I'm going to get packed, then I'm coming with you while this gets sorted out. Don't argue with me," she said to stop Addy's sputtering. "I'm staying with you at your place for double protection. I might not be a secret hitman, but I can handle myself with a Taser. And I've had some self-defense training. All those years modeling taught me not to trust men."

"Is that where you learned it?" Addy feigned innocence. "I thought it was a birth defect."

"Ha ha."

"Solene, I don't want you getting hurt."

"Hey, I've already had the baby stay with me. I'm on somewhat-speaking terms with Deacon. And I'm your best friend. I'd say I'm already involved. What's to stop whoever is after Noel from coming after me too?" A stretch, but hey, why not? Solene had no problem dealing with psychos, government sanctioned or not. But Addy was softer, not as aggressive. She was too damn nice. "It's settled. Now, help me pack."

And Deacon, when you get back, you and I are going to talk.

NINE

Except for a brief visit Saturday night, when he'd come over to thoroughly check over her house for security, Addy didn't see Noel the rest of the weekend.

She needed time to think. After sending Deacon over Sunday morning to make sure she was still okay, Noel hadn't bothered her except to tell her to let him know if she needed anything at all.

Solene settled into the spare bedroom with ease. She filled the lonely silence with chatter and jokes at Deacon's expense that made dealing with the aftermath of the weekend bearable.

Life on Monday seemed too normal, by contrast. The children in her class acted squirrely, typical for a Monday. She had chicken tacos for lunch, graded papers during their quiet reading time, and watched them all leave for home with a smile and wave. Then she drove to Solene's daycare and waited in the office, grading more papers, while her friend wrapped up to leave for the day.

"Okay, Marge has close-out," Solene announced as she popped her head in the doorway. "She and Annie are good. We can go."

They grabbed their coats and drove back to Addy's house. Once inside, she started a fire while Solene turned on the television and relaxed. Then Addy texted Noel that she'd returned from school.

He'd asked that she text him a few times a day so he knew she was all right. And since he'd been staying away, presumably to make her feel safer, away from memories of Seattle, she had no problem letting him know her status.

But the time apart also bothered her, because she missed him.

"I'm going to pop over to Noel's for a minute."

Solene raised her head and stared. "Oh?"

"Yes, I want to talk to him."

"So call him."

Addy knew Solene was trying to protect her. The way Noel was trying to protect her. "You know, I'm an adult. I can walk next door on my own, making my own choices in life."

Solene flushed. "Sorry. I worry about you. You're not jaded enough for twenty-six."

Addy chuckled. "And you're too jaded for thirty-four."

"Try thirty, bitch." Solene snorted. "Thirty-four, my ass."

Addy shook her head, grinning, and texted Noel about coming over. He replied with a yes right away. So that was a good sign, right?

Just give me ten minutes, he texted a moment later.

Just as she readied to leave, someone knocked at the door. Solene tensed, but Addy knew someone meaning to kill her wouldn't politely knock or ask to come in. He'd wait in the shadows and strangle her. At the thought, she rubbed her neck and hesitantly peered out the side window.

Seeing Deacon, she relaxed and opened the door.

He strolled through, carrying the baby in one arm, a neon green and orange striped diaper bag in the other.

"That's a very manly bag, Deacon," she said, trying not to laugh.

He made a face. "I know. But it was either this or pink monkeys." He shuddered. "I mean, I can be manly and fatherly at the same time. Why aren't there plaid or non-pastel striped bags out there for guys, right, Noel Jr.?"

The baby glanced around with wide eyes and grunted.

"That means yes." He winked at her. "Noel is waiting for you. I'm going to hang with my favorite blonde while you guys talk. You can cut through the side fence. He installed a gate yesterday just for you." His wide smile showed his amusement. "Noel is warming up, Addy. Nice work."

"Huh?"

"Nothing." He walked inside and gave Solene a big, insincere grin. "Solene Hansen, as I live and breathe. You get prettier each time I see you."

"Condescending ass," Solene muttered loudly enough to be heard. "What the hell are you doing here?"

"Solene, the baby." Deacon shook his head. "Go on, Addy. I'll keep the bobble-head company."

Solene shot off the couch. "The *what?*"

"So touchy. I meant him." He nodded down at the baby, whose head did seem to bobble around on that tiny neck. "You, dearest Solene, are nothing less than breathtaking."

"You got that right." Solene shook her blonde hair, and the effect was spectacular.

Addy saw Deacon try not to look impressed and fail.

Solene winked at her. "Be good, Addy."

"No, be bad," Deacon encouraged. "Noel needs a break. Dude is missing you something fierce, but you didn't hear that from me."

Addy left the house feeling lighter than she had in days. Noel really did like her. He missed her maybe, too. As much as she missed him? She hoped so.

It didn't seem possible to care for someone in so little time, but it felt as if she'd been given a taste of the real man under the aloof shell, only to have it ripped away before she could get to know him. And that hurt.

She knocked on his side door and waited for him to answer. The evening settled in, and the sky lost its bright blue color under the encroaching pink and orange blanket behind indigo clouds. The day looked magical.

Noel opened the door. He appeared the same as before, tan slacks, a button-down shirt, bare feet, she noted. But the sparkle in his eyes as he surveyed her made him seem more alive.

"Addy." He stepped back. "Come in."

"Hi, Noel." She passed him and did her best not to shiver. She could feel him watching her.

She jumped when she felt his hands on her shoulders.

"Can I take your coat?"

"Oh. Sure." She gave a half laugh and let him ease the jacket from her.

"You look nice."

She glanced down at her long skirt, boots, and favorite green cashmere sweater. It provided warmth while flattering her shape. "My teacher clothes. Thanks. Timmy Johnson likes it too."

"Timmy Johnson?"

"He's very cute and just turned nine. Oh, and he has a loose tooth."

Noel gave her one of his rare smiles. "Scared me for a minute there. I thought I had competition." His smile faded. "Addy, are you okay?"

She nodded. "It's been hard to forget, but I know you did what you had to do to save me."

He stepped closer and reached out, then lowered his hand to his side. "I would never, *ever*, do anything to hurt you. You have to believe that."

The raw expression on his face reassured her. "I know." She closed the distance between them and drew him down for a kiss.

The brief contact wasn't long enough. Then Noel did something that stirred her, deep inside. He tucked her head into his shoulder and hugged her. The warmth from the contact and his slow sigh melted her resistance.

"God, I missed you. It was only a couple of days, but it felt like forever. Give us a chance, okay? I can be a safe bet. I swear. I just need to work out a few kinks first."

She couldn't help the desperate laugh that left her. "A few kinks? The ones with guns, you mean."

"Yeah." He rubbed her back, and she loved the affectionate gesture. Noel offered comfort, not a seduction, and the difference meant something to her.

"Noel?"

"Yes?"

She pulled back to look into his dark eyes. When he stroked a finger down her cheek, another burst of emotion heated her belly. So much feeling for this man, and so much of it more than sexual. "Can we play cards again?"

He blinked, then smiled. "Sure."

"And this time you answer my questions, no matter who wins."

"If that's what you want." He hugged her again. "Anything for you, Addy."

The name of the game—Go Fish.

"I don't think I've played this in over twenty years."

Addy grinned. "I'm the master. I beat Ginny and Delia Anderson just last week, and those twins are practically psychic. Ha. Give me all your twos, sucker."

Noel just looked at her as he handed over three twos.

"I win again." Their third game.

He sighed. "What now?"

She'd been question loading on each win. "Well, I know your favorite color is green. You have a thing for Asian chicks."

"I never said that." He flushed. So adorable.

"You like me."

"You're not Asian. I mean, you are, partly, but it's not a race thing. I'm into you." He turned brighter red. "Never mind."

For someone so mysterious, once she'd gotten him talking about himself, Addy found him sweet and caring. But she'd had to dig deep to get to him. Though he'd said she could ask him anything, he'd been giving her stilted and shallow answers for half an hour. Only when she'd threatened to go home to check on Solene had he tempted her with deeper truths.

"Hmm, what else? You prefer guns to knives or poisons. You hate oppression of any kind. You especially hate people who are mean to kids and pets. You like dogs over cats, and you hate to cook."

"I don't think I'd say *hate*. I'd much rather gather the ingredients and let someone else put them together."

"That's okay. I love to cook."

His slow smile had the butterflies inside her doing somersaults.

"But what I really want to know…"

"Yes?"

"Were you serious before? In the hotel? You said you wanted me in all ways." An allusion to that kinky sex he'd requested. "Do you still?"

He tensed and slowly put his cards down. "Do you really have to ask?" He glanced down at himself.

She followed his gaze and saw the erection straining at his pants. Heat blazed within her.

"Addy, I want you any way I can have you. And yes, to answer your question, I want your ass in the worst way. I've been dreaming about taking you there. Hell, about having you under me again. We never got to finish that date." He dimmed a little. "I still blame myself for not taking better care of you. I'll never forget the look on your face when I found you. That bastard hurt you, and I wasn't there to stop that."

"He barely touched me." She leaned closer and put a hand on his cheek. "Noel, it wasn't your fault. This mess belongs to whoever is trying to hurt you. I understand your responsibilities. Remember, my dad was a cop. He put bad guys away all the time. Once in a while that spilled over to Mom and me. We stayed at my aunt's a time or two while Dad dealt with the threat. Mom never blamed him. And neither did I."

"But I'm not a cop. I kill people, Addy." He looked upset, which for Noel was saying something. "For all you know, I really am one of the bad guys. I'm sorry, but there's no one you can call to confirm what I told you. They can't know that you know. Not officially."

She didn't understand all that, but she did know the truth when she heard it. "I believe you, Noel. And I'm okay with what you are."

"Do you mean that?" He scooped her into his lap in seconds and just held her there, his chin on top of her head.

"Addy, I don't want to pressure you. But my feelings for you are deep. They have been for a long time, but I wouldn't let myself acknowledge them."

She smiled. "You're the only man who makes my heart race when he's near. The only guy who's ever made me so crazy I forgot all about protection when he was inside me. And you're the only one I've stalked for two years." She met his surprised gaze when he glanced down at her. "Did you ever wonder how I'd be on your doorstep whenever you got home? You stayed away for weeks, sometimes months, but I was always there when you came back. I, um, well, I kept an eye out for you."

"You did?" He beamed. "Damn."

"Solene thinks I'm nuts. So did I. But I wanted to know more about you. You're so sexy, in a somber, assassin-like kind of way."

"Shut up." His cheeks were pink.

"And you're so shy one minute, so domineering the next. I loved being with you in Seattle. And I know you'll always keep me safe."

His eyes filled with an emotion she didn't dare name. Not yet, because she wanted it so much. To be loved the way she loved him. To lighten the mood, she plucked at his shirt button, satisfied when he followed the movement without blinking.

"So, Noel, when are we going to finish our date?"

"Soon, very soon," he said, his voice husky. "But for now, what say we have a little refresher?" Noel turned her on his lap and had her straddle his waist. He put a hand on her belly and slid it under her skirt and panties, seeking the heat of her. "Damn. You're wet."

She refused to be left behind. So she unbuttoned and unzipped his fly, then pushed beneath his underwear to grip him. "And you're hard and hot."

He groaned and thrust into her hand. "I want inside you."

"No condom?"

"No condom," he agreed, then groaned. "Fuck. No condom." Noel only swore when he was on the edge.

Just like her right now. "How about we play instead, sexy?"

He nodded, staring at her while he slid his fingers over her wet folds, priming her as he rubbed her clit. Then he pumped a finger inside her and added another.

"Let's see who comes first," he challenged, his voice thick.

"Oh, let's." She couldn't help moving over him, wanting more of that pleasurable pressure. While she did, she gripped him, sliding her hand up and down and giving him as much tension as she could around that thick shaft. He was so big, so hard. She loved feeling how she affected him. And the slick feel of his cockhead told her he was close.

"Come for me, Addy." He watched her, and knowing he saw all her pleasure increased her arousal.

"Come for *me,* Noel." She pumped faster, felt him drawing closer, and shared in his desire. Her moans and pants mirrored his, until they were both groaning and striving for that ultimate release.

"Yes, baby. Coming," he growled and shoved his fingers deeper inside her.

That action set him off, and he came while she clamped around his fingers, her spasms making it hard to breathe while she climaxed with her lover.

They sat together, joined in release, and stared into each other's eyes.

"Addy."

"Noel."

He smiled. "Only with you."

"Yes, baby." She knew he liked it when she called him that. She held him tighter, and he flexed and moaned as he spurted again. "Only with you."

Once they cleaned up, he walked her back home. "We have to finish our first date," he reminded her. "How about Wednesday night?"

"Will Deacon watch Griffith for you?"

He chuckled. "That poor kid has got the worst names to choose from. But yeah, I'll make—I mean, *ask*—Deacon to watch his baby while I get inside my girlfriend's pants."

"So romantic, Noel."

They both laughed.

Then she asked, "Is that what I am? Your girlfriend?"

"You're so much more than that. My girlfriend, my lover. You're it for me, Addy. I don't want to scare you off, but I'm not into games. When this mess is over, I want us to be together. Just thought you should know."

He kissed her at the door, then nudged her inside when she stared at him in shock.

He wants us to be together?

"Yo, Deacon, quit arguing with Solene. Let's go." Noel tapped her chin. "Close your mouth, Addy. And don't worry. I'm going to give you time to get used to the idea. Once I'm done with work, I'll be living on the island full time. So I can be patient."

"Patient? For what?" Solene asked, coming behind them.

Deacon took the baby from her and whistled as he left.

Noel kissed Addy before following Deacon.

Solene pulled her inside. "What's going on?"

"Noel and I are dating. And I think, I mean, I could be wrong, but I think he just asked me to marry him. Without asking me to marry him." She paused in thought. "But he never actually mentioned marriage or love. He just said he wanted us to be together. What the hell does that mean?"

"Hmm. That's pretty slick. Sounds to me like you want to get married to Mr. Murder. Before you left, you were on pins and needles about your killer boyfriend. Now everything's perfect?" Solene groaned. "You people are giving me a headache. Men. Blech. I can't handle any more. I'm going to bed."

Addy blinked. "It's six o'clock."

"I'm taking a bubble bath then," Solene snapped. "And *you're* making dinner. I stayed here with Sir Annoys-a-Lot while you and Noel made up. The only thing saving you from a real tongue-lashing is that I'm half in love with that baby. He is *sooo* cute. Still not worth dealing with Deacon. But whatever. I'm tired. I'm annoyed. Oh, and I'm glad you're happy. Now I'm going to soak. Call me when dinner's ready."

Addy watched Solene stalk away and practically danced into the kitchen. Noel loved her—didn't he? She could feel it. He had to feel that closeness if he wanted forever with her. Did he want that? She did. Addy envisioned marriage and babies and a white picket fence—around that house next door.

She continued to dream about Noel while she fixed a salad and chicken.

But reality intruded once more when she noticed the baby bottle Deacon had forgotten to take with him.

Noel might be the father of another woman's child. The mother had left the boy behind, but that was no guarantee she would never return. And what about Noel's past? He wanted out of his current job. Would they let him go? What would Noel do here? She had no idea what his finances might be like. Just because they were hot in the sack and out of it, the real world, devoid of travel and glamor, might wear thin after a while.

And he'd never said he loved her.

She had a lot to think about. The least of which would be her date on Wednesday night, when they got down and dirty and made the rest of her fantasies come true.

She snorted. *Real life can wait. He said he'd be patient. Well, I want my dreams to come true while we're sorting out the rest.* Yes, much better to prioritize sex and the now over a future that might never come to be.

The pragmatic teacher in her made plans, and Addy smiled to herself as she realized that in order to make things work with Noel, she'd have to lead him there. They'd play by her rules.

He might know the ins and outs of a pistol, but she knew how to handle a man afraid of love.

TEN

Noel walked back with a whistling Deacon and a giggling baby.

"You know, he's a happy guy," Deacon was saying about the infant. "Of course, wrapped up in soft arms and against Solene's rack, I'm sure I'd be happy too." He snorted. "Damn woman is a hothead, but she's finer than shit. You know?"

Noel had been half-listening. "What?"

Deacon frowned. "Why are you wearing different pants?"

"Oh, I spilled something on them." More like he'd left a stain on them, but Deacon didn't need the details. Just the thought of how Addy had handled him made him hard again. Hell, the woman could breathe and he grew aroused. Then to learn she'd been looking for him for the past few years while he'd been checking up on her?

They were made for each other. He must have done something right with his life to have Addy as a reward.

"Hey, genius. Stop daydreaming about your girlfriend and take the kid. I think he needs a change."

Deacon handed over the baby and hotfooted it inside the house.

Noel smelled the truth of the matter and hurried to the changing table in the spare room. "Geez, kid. You stink." He set the boy down and removed the diaper, doing his best not to gag. He'd gotten pretty good at changing diapers. Without Deacon or Hammer for a break, he'd in fact started to grow attached to the well-tempered baby.

Said baby grabbed for his finger and smiled.

Noel's heart pounded as he stared down and smiled back. "Am I your father?" he whispered. As far-fetched as the idea seemed, he wasn't so opposed to it anymore. A future with Addy and babies felt right.

No more killing. No more destruction. Here he could build a life. His garden, his girlfriend, his future. But without the Business, he didn't know what he'd do for a living. With the amount of money he'd earned and his investments, he never had to work again. The one huge perk for contract work—it paid extremely well. Since most contractors didn't make it past the first year, Noel, Deacon, and Hammer were considered pros in their field.

"I'm leaving my job," he told the baby, who squirmed on the table.

Quickly disposing of the diaper in a nearby container and cleaning the baby before re-diapering him, he stared down at the little guy. "Time to start new. Maybe you could stay with me and Addy. We could be a family."

Family.

The word felt rusty on his tongue. He had hazy recollections of his parents before the car crash that had ended everything.

Fights between his father and mother. A happiness all too normal, because it had been fleeting. They loved each other, but his parents had been very different. She'd wanted more children, to settle down. He'd been married to his job, traveling, and making good money forecasting for businesses. They'd been apart more than they'd been together, but Noel had always looked forward to his father's return.

His father hadn't wanted children in the first place, but he'd loved Noel. Had been fond of his wife as well, though Noel had sensed the friction between them, had heard the accusations of infidelity.

The car crash had been a fluke. A slick road, bad weather, and a flooded river. Only by some miracle had he not been swept up in the flood as well, rescued by a group of firemen already close by trying to save a stray dog stranded in the roaring waters.

Noel had tried to overcome his grief by being a stellar

student, never getting in trouble. But an abusive foster family hadn't helped.

Then he'd been on his own, living on the streets. There he'd met Big Joe's predecessor, a burly man with notions of right and wrong, and odd ideas of how to fix all the bad in the world.

That man had seen something in Noel. The way he'd seen something in Deacon and Hammer and all the others recruited young into the Business.

Noel felt a sense of loyalty, yes, but he'd given them enough.

He heard Deacon's footsteps.

"Is it safe?" Deacon entered and sniffed. "Mostly safe, I think."

Noel lifted the now clean baby in his arms. He didn't feel awkward holding such innocence anymore. He felt protective. "Deacon?"

"Yeah?" Deacon lifted light gray eyes to his, that gaze seeing far more than many would suspect. Noel knew Deacon liked to be thought of as shallow, charming, basic. But the man was much more, a keen intellect who studied and dissected problems with ease.

"I'm leaving."

Deacon watched him. "Leaving…?"

"The Business. I'm done."

Deacon said nothing, studying him. "Is this because of the baby?"

"No. It's been a while in coming." He heard a yawn and put the baby to his shoulder, patting him softly on the back, as he'd seen Addy do. "I know what we do matters. That we help make the world a better place. But I'm tired of killing. I want more than that. I want to plant my boring vegetables." He saw Deacon's lips quirk. "Watch the sunset from one place, not from a different port in a different country each night. I want to know I'm building something, not just taking something or someone down."

Deacon stared at the back of the baby's head. "You know, I get it. Those of us who do this work understand like no one else can."

"Yes."

"I think about it too. About leaving. But I have nothing else. It's not that I like killing people. Though I admit it's sometimes satisfying. I don't have that problem with right and wrong like you do, Noel. Ice. You're cold because you think it's wrong to fix problems the way we do. But I don't. I love living in the gray." He smiled, but the expression stopped short of his eyes. "Sometimes doing all the right things the right way won't solve a problem. They need us, Noel."

"Yes, but they don't need *me* anymore. I'm done, Deacon."

"I understand. But do you think Big Joe will?"

"I hope he does. I'd hate to kill him to prove a point." He

nestled the baby against him as he tensed, hoping like hell it wouldn't come to that.

"You have a baby to protect."

"Deacon, we both know there's a strong possibility this baby is yours."

"Or Hammer's," Deacon was quick to point out. He sighed. "I know, man. Honestly, I'm tired of all of the shit too." He looked into Noel's eyes. "It's easier talking about it with someone who understands. You and Hammer. This kid." Deacon grinned. "We're friends now, aren't we, Noel? Kinda like family, even."

Noel grimaced. "I guess so."

Deacon laughed, then lowered his voice when they saw the baby drift off. "That's good. Friends are good. I'm a loyal kind of guy. So's Hammer. Unless you fuck us over, we'll stand by you and the kid." He nodded to the baby. "We're the good ones, the ones who know when too much brutality is too much. There are a lot of guys in the Business who don't know when to quit. Big Joe will let you off, Noel. I'll make sure of it."

Noel couldn't believe his good fortune. Unless Deacon was dicking with him. "Don't lie to me, because I'll know."

"Nah, you won't. I'm good at what I do." Deacon grinned. "I'm not lying about this, though. That kid is special. Something good that came from one of us. I swear to you the kid will be okay. One way or the other."

Noel nodded. "Good. The thing that still bothers me is we have nothing on the mother. Hammer still hasn't learned anything."

"Damn. I picked up some interesting ideas while you were gone. Aside from knowing what diapers and wipes work best with the stink-butt"—he nodded at the baby—"I can tell you that someone out there hates you, me, and Hammer."

"I get Wilkes hating me because I killed his brother." Ted, the fake meth head with the botched attempted mugging. "But all three of us?" Noel glanced at the baby again and continued to rock him. "So the baby is connected to the attempts to kill me?"

"I can't say for certain, but I think so." Deacon grabbed a notepad out of the back pocket of his jeans. "I was going to wait for Hammer to get back to share this, but what the hell. What else do we have to do?"

"Hold on." Noel set the baby down in the crib Deacon had purchased while he was gone. "Nice crib, by the way."

Deacon shrugged. "At least now I'm not worried he'll roll off the bed. Kid wriggles like an eel."

Noel left the baby after turning on the baby monitor. Deacon followed him into the kitchen, where Noel turned on the other monitor and put a kettle on for some hot chocolate.

"Want some?" he asked.

Deacon brightened. "Do you have mini-marshmallows?"

"No, the big ones. They didn't have any tiny ones at the store or I'd have gotten some."

"Bummer, but okay."

Noel saw the humor in two grown-ass men who killed for a living bonding over hot chocolate and marshmallows. "So, what did you learn?"

"That there's rumor of a plant living on the island, keeping watch. Our guy, I think. That the hits on you were to shake you up, to see if you could handle yourself on your down-time. Someone's been following you and knows your habits. Not good, Noel."

"Damn."

"But we both know the only people who know where you live, who know who you are, come from the Business. I had a friend in admin do some quiet research for me. Four names popped up. Hammer's one, for that mix-up in Madrid. But I don't think he's in on this at all. He's one of us."

"Is he?" Hammer had been quiet while on his trip to Penn-sylvania. Maybe too quiet? "That excursion to Madrid cost the Business two agents and nearly had me and Hammer killing each other." A rogue handler had tried to take out several contractors, Hammer and Noel being two of them. Only Noel's keen sense that something was off had kept him from shooting Hammer. Hammer had seen the truth and backed down as well, questioning orders when others would have simply pulled the trigger.

"Yes. I'd stake my life on it." Deacon nodded. "But the other three names are potentials."

"Who are they?"

"We have another we can scratch off. The Prince had a problem with me and Hammer in Mexico. You remember Jonas Hood?"

Noel thought for a moment. "Oh, right. He was better looking than you are and more skilled with the ladies." And a man who'd always put Noel on edge. Jonas had been one of the contractors who seemed to revel in death and destruction.

"Bullshit." Deacon scowled.

Noel smirked. "Whatever you say. But Jonas died in a fire during the Diablo Blanco Cartel bust. That had nothing to do with me or you two. Did it?"

"No. But he died, so he's off the list. Though he might have had friends who could have blamed us if they had the right intel. I did have contacts in Sinaloa at the time. I could have prevented Jonas's death if I'd been told. Not that that's the case, but it could be made to look like I didn't care."

"Something to look into. The other two names?" The kettle whistled, and Noel poured the water. As he and Deacon stirred their hot chocolate, they both eyed the marsh-mallow bag.

"Five left. Three for me, two for you," Deacon suggested. No question of splitting that last.

"Yeah, right. My house. I get three."

"I'll shoot you for it."

Noel raised a brow.

"I meant in the basement. We shoot for the last one."

"You know you can't beat me with a gun. A knife, maybe. Not a pistol." He tapped his Jericho, which remained tucked in his belt holster at all times—*when I'm not with Addy, that is.*

"Shit. Fine. Have it."

But Deacon looked so dejected, Noel handed it to him. "Baby."

"Waaa." Deacon bit into the treat and sighed. "Ah, this is the life."

Noel shook his head. "The names?"

"Oh, right. Burleigh and Vasquez. Burleigh, you remember, is a British expat who hates your guts."

"The rapist." Noel seethed, remembering Burleigh's favorite pastime—hurting underage girls in the name of "gathering information."

"He hates that name." Deacon chuckled. "He earned it, but

still. Because of us, he was let go and had to hide for fear of getting the 'axe'."

"The bastard."

"Well, hear-tell he still hates the three of us. So even though he's been living it up in Jaipur, I think he'd be happy to kill us all slowly."

"I agree, except the sloppy nature of the hits isn't his style."

"Yeah, that bugs me too. Plus, he wouldn't know where you go when you're not at work. The house isn't in your name, and you don't file taxes. There is no Noel Ridgemont anywhere but in Washington, D.C." A false trail the Business had for all their employees. Fake last names and fake addresses of record. "And you know he's hated by everyone in admin. Rape ain't pretty by any means, and especially not to the ladies working with our files."

"Right. So our last possibility?"

"This one makes the most—and least—amount of sense. Angelina Vasquez."

Noel paused from dumping his marshmallows in his cocoa. "The Angel. Also dead. The same name in a locket sent with the baby. A code, a name, the locket, a baby. And attempts on my life. You know, they have to be related."

"Yeah, but how? She's been a ghost for years. If only we had a face to put with the name. The only thing we know for sure is she's female."

"Addy saw her," Noel said.

"True, but that description she gave us accounts for anyone with dark hair and dark eyes. For all we know, the mother used some random woman to drop off the baby."

Noel nodded, thinking. "We know for a fact Addy and Solene are who they say they are." Neither of them could be Angel.

"Exactly."

Noel had checked and rechecked Addy's credentials years ago, especially when he'd felt such an attraction to her. Anyone associated with her got the same scrutiny. Solene was an ex-model turned entrepreneur. Addy's ex-boyfriends and dates had also panned out.

Noel was missing something. "I don't like any of this."

"Neither do I." Deacon frowned. "Solene's a major pain in the ass, and she's in danger by association now. It's too late now to back her out. Or Addy for that matter. Let's hope Hammer has something more definite for us when he gets back. *If* he gets back." Deacon took out his phone and scrolled through it. "Where is that jackass?"

"He's in Maryland right now, or so he said a few hours ago."

"And he couldn't tell *me* that?" Deacon swore. "What a dick. And who made you boss of our little group?"

Noel dumped the marshmallows in his mug and took a satisfying drink. "Ah. What do you mean who put me in charge? I'm a natural leader. You're our ace intelligence-gatherer. You, who can charm the pants off of anyone." Except Solene, apparently. Interesting she bothered Deacon so much. "We both know Hammer isn't known for his subtlety. He's the muscle."

"I guess. But I don't have to like it." Deacon swigged his cocoa. "Man, this is good stuff. Much better than that cheap crap. Okay, it's decided. Your place remains HQ until we see this through. I like your food."

"Gee, I'm so glad. I hadn't thought that was up for debate." Noel gave Deacon a glare. "Oh, and on that note, you're babysitting on Wednesday. At Addy's house. You can keep an eye on Solene while Addy and I finish our date."

"Finish, huh?" Deacon gave him a sly grin. "I'd say you finished earlier, if you get my meaning."

Noel refused to grace that comment with an answer.

"Truth hurts, huh? Well at least you're getting some action. I'm dry as dust lately."

But not for lack of offers. Noel had seen Deacon wield that smile with deadly efficiency. "What? Solene not impressed by your charms?"

"Not yet. Woman is stubborn, annoying, and a know-it-all."

"And too pretty for you, is that it?"

"Maybe." Deacon finished off his drink. "But she's not so

nice, so there's that. Your teacher is way too good for you, Ice."

"I know. But I'm keeping her anyway." *I think. Hell, I hope.*

"Does she know that?"

"Kind of."

Deacon laughed. "Watching you try to charm your way into her good graces would be fun if I wasn't so busy babysitting. Fine, you get Wednesday night. But I want a favor in return."

"What?"

"I don't know yet."

"Great." Noel sighed. "Let's hope Hammer's having more luck than we are with this." He glanced at Deacon. "So… You ever think of seriously leaving the Business?"

"Sure. Who hasn't? But what else would I do? I'm good at it, and I'm not into gardening or sunsets. I'd be bored living the good life." Deacon kidded him, but Noel thought he heard a hint of longing in his friend's voice.

"Who knows? Maybe we can find you something to do on the island. I hear Solene can always use a hand at the daycare."

"I'd rather lose another pair of jeans to stink-butt again."

"DID YOU DO IT, NINE?"

"Yes. He's out and has his directions. He'll do it, no question. I paid him in advance."

"Outstanding work." He nodded. Pleased. The plans had come together so nicely. He hadn't expected Noel to find the woman so quickly, or to dispatch Rene in front of her. But having done so had surely put a wedge between them. Adeline Rose couldn't possibly like being near a killer.

He knew more about her than anyone would think. How sweet and kind she was. How she treasured her school children. Even her bitch of a friend, one who might yet serve him if she played her cards right.

He had a place for a woman with Solene Hansen's looks and fire. Oh yes.

With a glance at his bedroom, where two women lay doping up, waiting for him to return and give them what only he could, he picked up a photograph, stared at it, then put it back in his desk drawer.

"I miss you, Angel. With any luck, you'll come back to me. But make no mistake. I'll have your heart. One way or the other."

And he planned to witness his enemies go down. He had a front row seat, after all.

ELEVEN

Wednesday evening, right before Noel's big date, Hammer returned. *Of course.* Worst possible timing, but what the hell? Noel had been having one of those days. The baby had just puked over his carefully chosen outfit, much to Deacon's amusement.

The bastard still hadn't stopped laughing.

Wilkes had disappeared before the clean-up crew had arrived, and no one knew how he'd gotten away, which was still preying on his mind. Addy had stayed late after school due to some plumbing issues in her classroom and was working with her principal and the maintenance crew to fix it, so their date had been pushed back another hour. And earlier in the afternoon, Solene had taken her lunch break at his house, despite not receiving an invite, and bitched him out thoroughly.

"I swear by all that's holy. You hurt Addy in any way, break her heart or her pinkie toe, even by accident, and I'll

make your life a living hell," she said, the words cold and concise. A threat by any measure, and one he knew to take to heart.

If Solene hadn't meant the world to Addy, he could have ignored the woman. But she was Addy's best friend, and she only had Addy's interests at heart. How could he not respect her for that?

"I treasure her. I'd never do anything to hurt her." He looked her in the eye. "And I'd never allow anyone else to hurt her, either."

She swallowed but didn't step back. A sure sign of courage, since she knew he could take her out between one breath and the next.

"Good." She nodded. "One more thing. Just because she and I are best friends doesn't mean we share everything. I am not *on the menu."*

That had surprised him, that she'd needed to tell him what he already knew. "I take it others have made the assumption?"

She grimaced. "Yeah. It was so skeevy, but I couldn't tell Addy because I didn't want to hurt her feelings. She hadn't been into the guy anyway, so it hadn't mattered. But she can be a little self-conscious about her looks sometimes."

"Addy?" He snorted. "You have to be kidding me. She's gorgeous."

Solene smiled. "Yes, she is. Okay, enough said. Now what do you have I can eat? Oh, and I'm a huge fan of carbs."

Noel had dealt with obstacles like that all day long, when he should have been focused on Addy. And here, another big one to overcome.

"What a trip." Hammer yawned. "I want nothing but a bed for the next twelve hours. I found out a few things, but I now have more questions than I did before I left."

"Yeah? Like what?" Deacon propped himself against Noel's dresser, the little guy in his arms and starting to fuss.

They stood in his bedroom watching him hunt for a new outfit, one not covered in baby vomit. "Can it keep?" Noel growled, needing to concentrate on his evening with Addy, not more bad news. He couldn't screw up with her again. He'd only get so many chances to convince the woman he wasn't a bad bet.

Deacon patted the baby on the back. "Come on, Hammer. Noel's getting ready to put it to his lady. We don't want to be here when that happens."

Hammer perked up. "Addy, right? His lady now? I go away for a few days and miss so much."

"I'll fill you in. And I'll get a pizza and beer if you keep that blonde barracuda off me while we babysit Noel Jr. We're staying overnight, right, Noel?"

"Hopefully."

Hammer grinned. "Cool. I've been thinking." The pair walked away with the baby while Noel continued his search. "How about we call him Monty? He's a cute kid, and I'm a great guy. We should name him after someone grand."

"You claiming him as yours?" Deacon asked, his voice growing fainter.

The door opened. "Not exactly, but—"

Noel didn't hear any more because they'd closed the door behind them. Much as he wanted to know what the hell Hammer had learned, it could wait. He had to calm his nerves, both excited and nervous about being with Addy again.

He had to get tonight perfectly right. He wanted her to feel so much pleasure, so much care, that she'd never want to leave him. Ever. Although he'd told her he wanted her after they cleaned up this mess, he didn't know if she'd change her mind. He was a killer. He had no one to recommend him, nothing but a great house and the promise of millions behind him. But Addy didn't know about his money, and she wasn't the type to like a man for his wealth. She needed a guy with heart—and his had been encased in ice for more than a decade.

He ran a hand over his denim button-down shirt and jeans. He hadn't worn shoes, because he didn't like them in the home messing his floors. Deacon and Hammer would have to break that habit, and soon, before he broke them.

After slapping on a bit of cologne and making sure every-thing remained neat and tidy, he double-checked his stash of lube and condoms in the drawer and smiled.

He'd show her a night she'd never forget.

AFTER PICKING up their dinner and setting it on nice plates, Noel chilled a bottle of wine and made sure they both had water to drink. The flowers and lit candles also added to the ambiance, and as he surveyed his handiwork, he thought he'd done a decent job.

He wanted tonight to be just for her. With the guys staying at Addy's with Solene, he had nothing but time for Addy.

A knock at the door drew his attention. He felt his palms sweat and had to laugh at himself. The last time he'd been this nervous, he'd been on his first contract. Since then, he'd been in his share of dangerous situations, some he hadn't expected to survive. Yet one pretty woman with bright green eyes and a heartwarming smile made him shake?

God, I'm pathetic.

Where had Ice gone, and should Noel even try to bring him back?

He opened the door and found a maintenance man with a clipboard on his doorstep.

Noel immediately recognized his mistake, taking for

granted Addy had been at the door. As if the danger had passed and wasn't waiting to take him again.

He prepared himself to snap the guy's neck before assessing the scene for other threats. *Stupid stupid.* He'd turned off the back alarm since the others had been accessing the back and side yards to come and go through the new gate to Addy's place.

The maintenance man glanced at the clipboard, then back at Noel in puzzlement. He didn't go for a weapon or make any sudden moves. "Ah, is Ms. Hansen home?"

"Solene?"

The guy glanced at his clipboard again. His nametag read Bob in bright red letters and he wore a gray-striped, collared work shirt. "Is this NE 2228? Solene Hansen called about a flooding dishwasher."

Noel relaxed, but not totally. "No. You want the house next door." He reached into his back pocket for his phone and realized he'd left it on the dining table. "Hold on."

He turned slowly, still feeling something off about the man at the door. But Bob didn't move while Noel grabbed his phone. Noel had just returned to the front door when he realized what bothered him about Bob's untimely arrival. "Where's your vehicle?"

Bob frowned and turned. "What the...? Son of a bitch!" Bob dropped his clipboard. "I parked it right there. I don't understand. What the hell is going on?"

Bob faced Noel again with a glare. "Are you screwing with me?"

"No."

Bob swore as he retrieved his clipboard from the ground. "Christ. This is all I need. I have to call my boss. Hold on." He reached behind himself.

Noel did the same, gripping the pistol at his back.

But Bob only retrieved his phone and dialed. "Jeff? Hey man, I have a problem. A weird fucking problem."

Noel eased his hand off the grip and brought his hands to his sides.

Bob continued to report about the theft of his van. "Yeah, I'm at—Hey, buddy. Can you tell me what address this is and who you are? I'm going to have to file a police report, but my boss wants to get this down too."

"NE 2224 Beach Comber. Name is Noel—"

The clipboard shot at his throat so fast Noel only had time to veer back and shift, taking the blow against his collarbone. Better that than his jugular, he thought through the sting. Bob brought his phone up and aimed at Noel's face.

Noel dropped, narrowly missing the electronic jolt that sizzled in the air. Not a phone after all, but a Taser. Furious with himself for lowering his guard when he knew better, he knocked the phone aside and straightened with an uppercut into his assailant's gut. He followed up with a knee to the man's face, a leg sweep, and stood over Bob, holding him in a wristlock to keep him on his back while the asshole bled over the porch with a broken nose.

"Who sent you?"

Bob wheezed. "Fuck you." A small sound behind him warned Noel to move. *Now.*

Tiny pops. Gravel in the driveway scattered, and lead thudded into the porch railing as silenced-rounds peppered the area. Noel darted behind an Adirondack chair, determining the shots to be coming from the driveway farther down. He didn't have a silencer on his pistol and didn't want to alarm anyone next door, so he wouldn't use his gun unless he had to.

Instead, he darted into the house and shut the door behind him. Then he grabbed his favorite knife from beneath the coffee table in the living room and turned off all the lights. He exited quietly through the back door.

Fortunately, the late hour and cloudy evening cut way down on ambient light. Noel listened for movement. Hearing a slight rustle from the shrubs in the way back, he stayed low, behind his greenhouse.

Not sure if the intruders had night-vision capability, he figured he'd be better off back inside. But patience normally proved the smarter way to go, so he crouched, still, and waited.

The muffled sound of footsteps through grass had him turn and face the back porch. Before long, he saw a figure in black start up the back porch stairs. Noel rushed the guy and buried the knife in the man's chest, Noel's hand over his mouth to prevent a scream. Unfortunately, this intruder didn't carry more than a knife and garrote with him. Needing to get back to Bob before the guy left, he hurried around to the front.

Bob was gone. Perhaps inside the house, hunting Noel?

Noel swore under his breath, knowing he needed to take care of this before Addy—God forbid—walked into the mess. He had a date to get ready for, and no amount of dead bodies would change that.

Which meant getting rid of unwanted house guests, dead or alive.

He listened cautiously, heard nothing, and let himself into a secret entrance next to his home, hidden by an overlarge shrub. He punched in a silent code, which allowed entry into his basement, where his shooting range, cache of weapons, and backup servers were stored.

After double-checking his clip, he flicked on the security cameras and looked for what didn't belong.

Ah, there. The enemy lingered in the baby's room.

That violation bothered him more than anything else that these men had done. It was one thing to go after him. Another to attack Addy, for which they'd pay dearly. But to taint such innocence, to go through the baby's room, that evil walking into a place that didn't belong...

Noel turned cold again, focused. He put a tiny metal ball in his pocket and moved on silent feet up the stairs, his gun at the ready. He entered his bedroom through a secret panel behind a bookcase. But he didn't want more blood in the house. So he stashed his sidearm close, in a nearby hidey-hole, and continued out into the hall toward the baby's room. Movement inside ceased.

Noel made his move. He rolled the small ball in the opposite direction down the hall.

Bob limped out of the room and aimed at the sound. In a flash, Noel had him in a headlock.

He could have choked him out, left him for Hammer or Deacon to handle. But Bob rasped, "Do whatever you want. That kid and that bitch will be ours soon enough. And they'll know pain—"

Noel didn't want to hear any more. He broke the fucker's neck and dropped him, then collected the man's gun. After picking up the other weapon from outside, he took a deep breath and let it out. Then he texted Deacon in code and explained the situation.

He didn't have long to wait. His cell phone rang immediately.

"Yes?" Noel asked.

"The fuck you say," Deacon swore. "You want me to plant *two* of them? Right now?"

"A garden is only as good as its fertilizer, Deacon. I can't risk my tomatoes. You know how much work I've put into my planting for today."

"Hammer can do it. I'm babysitting." Deacon disconnected.

Minutes later, Hammer appeared at the backdoor, a tarp in hand. "You rang?"

ADDY SWALLOWED AROUND A DRY THROAT. She couldn't say why she was so nervous, except tonight seemed like a turning point in her relationship with Noel. She pulled into his driveway and parked. He'd told her that they'd have the house to themselves while Deacon and Solene babysat.

She turned off the ignition and pulled down the visor mirror, studying her reflection. Despite the mess at work with a leak in the bathroom that had almost spilled through to her room, the janitorial staff had managed to clean it up while she and the principal discussed a few disciplinary actions with students she'd been meaning to talk about for some time. With parent-teacher conferences coming soon, she'd been glad to get that matter straightened out.

But it had burned that she'd had to postpone her time with Noel even more.

She stepped out of her car and knew she looked good. The long, navy-blue skirt made her look taller, and the white silk blouse caressed her slender torso and emphasized the gentle roundness of her breasts. Plus, the shirt set off the deep black of her hair. She'd gone all-out on eyeliner and lipstick too, her hair poker-straight and brushed to within an inch of its life.

She could to do this. Do Noel.

Addy grinned. It felt important that she make the moves tonight. To accept Noel sexually and emotionally, and to get him to commit to her. Granted, their courtship had been whirlwind supersonic, but she knew him. Her vulnerable assassin had been on tenterhooks with her since the shooting. Had he been blasé or cocky, she might have been too scared to be with him again.

But he'd gone right back to being Noel. A bit of a take-charge kind of guy, but so gentle with the baby, with her.

She couldn't stop thinking about all their night might have been. Had she ever felt so taken care of before? So well-pleasured?

She walked up the steps to his porch and noted a stain. He'd hate that. She'd mention it later, once she determined his mood. Addy rang the bell and waited.

He answered quick enough, wearing khaki pants and a denim button-down shirt and socks. His bright smile welcomed her, as did the tug to pull her into his arms.

"Ah, I was waiting for this." The slow, sweet kiss had her heart racing. "Come on in, Addy. You're in for a treat."

She toed off her heels and joined him in the kitchen. The

dining table looked fabulous, all decked out with pretty dinnerware, flowers, and candles. "Okay, I'm impressed."

"And we haven't even gotten to the food yet."

Addy wanted to smile, to joke, but her nerves wouldn't let her. He wanted them to *eat dinner?* She had no intention of messing up her clean system, not when she'd been sucking down water all day, preparing her body for a bit of anal play.

She'd read the horror stories when it came to anal sex. And the one and only time she'd tried it she'd been so nervous she'd make a mess or that it would hurt, it had done little for her enjoyment. Then again, the regular sex with good old Mike hadn't been stellar either. She knew with Noel the experience would be different.

She walked toward him, pleased to see caution in his eyes. "How about another kiss first?"

He smiled. "That I can do." He waited for her to reach him, then sagged back into the counter and hugged her, spreading his feet so she could stand between them. "I missed you, Addy."

"Me too," she sighed then kissed him. Time for the kid gloves to come off. Nothing soft or light about the kiss she laid on him. Addy threw herself into it and took advantage until she lost her breath.

She pulled back to see him staring down at her with intense, dark eyes. Then he was back, taking charge and kissing her while pressing a huge erection against her belly.

Bingo. The motherlode.

She dragged her mouth to his cheek, his ear, and whispered, "I don't want to wait. We can eat…after. I want you inside me now."

He groaned and gripped her waist while she angled a hand between them and caressed the steel-hard rod in his pants.

"I think you want me right back," she breathed.

"You know I do." He squeezed her hips. "You sure, honey? Because once we get started, I don't think I'll be able to stop for appetizers."

She chuckled and pumped his cock. "Oh, I'm sure. I've had a hard day. Not as hard as yours, I'm sure."

His dry laugh caught her off guard.

"What am I missing?"

"Oh, I'll tell you later. Much later." He carried her down the hall to his bedroom. Of course, it would have felt more romantic if he hadn't slung her over a shoulder to carry her, but she'd take what she could get.

He tossed her onto the bed and dragged off his clothing.

She frowned. "Is that a bruise?" A dark mark lined the right side of his collarbone.

"Maybe. Training."

Huh. She hadn't thought about that. A man in Noel's profession had to keep in shape.

"I'll answer the million questions I can see forming in that teacher brain later. Right now, I need you."

"Yes, you do." She pulled her skirt higher, showing off her thigh-high stockings and lacy thong.

"Oh, baby." Noel stood naked and erect, more than ready for what she had planned.

She spread her legs and bent her knees, flattening her feet on the bed. Then she unbuttoned her shirt and unfastened her matching lace bra by its front clasp. All white, yet she wouldn't claim to be innocent.

Noel's gaze burned as it trailed over her. "Who needs steak when I have this?"

"Wait. Did you say *steak*?" She laughed when he pounced, but she wasn't laughing anymore when he sucked her nipple and toyed her into a heavy arousal. He palmed one breast while licking the other, and before she knew it, he'd removed her shirt, bra, and panties, leaving her in only her skirt and stockings.

He continued to teethe, and the bites over her sensitive nipples threw her into a deep arousal.

"Yes, Noel. Oh yeah," she moaned and gripped his hair, needing him to stop caressing her ribs and belly and move lower. "I'm so wet."

"Good." He sounded guttural, but he didn't stop playing

with her.

He leaned up and mounted her, no condom that she'd seen, but she didn't care. The skirt bunched around her waist, but rubbing her stocking-clad legs against Noel felt sinful.

"In me."

"Oh baby. We're going to play tonight, Adeline Rose. I'll make you feel so fucking good." Noel rarely cursed. He must really be into her. "Don't worry. I won't come in your pussy." He smiled, and a dangerous man stared at her. All that ferocity and need amped her desire. She had a tiger by the tail, and she knew it.

"Where will you come?" she asked, then gasped when he shoved inside her in one slick push.

"In that ass. I can't wait to fill you up." He fucked her, hard, but when she felt her release growing too close, he withdrew and left her aching.

Noel slid down her body and yanked her skirt free, leaving her in nothing but her stockings. "You'll have to wear these for me again."

"Yes." Whatever he wanted, he could have. If he'd just let her climb back up that path to ecstasy once more.

But her contract man had no intention of playing nice, apparently. And she fell straight up in love with the riveted killer staring at nothing but her.

TWELVE

Noel wanted to go easier on her, but lust rode him hard. Sinking inside her without a condom had been incredible. He'd fucked her, had felt her perfect body gloving him, and nearly come too soon.

Now he had to seduce the woman who'd already seduced him. Addy had nearly fried his circuits with that kiss in the kitchen. He'd wanted the romance and the candlelight to erase the negative energy from before. Killing in the house he wanted to woo his lady in didn't seem right.

But this? Fucking Addy, making love to his woman, at her insistence?

"That's right. Spread those legs wider." She hadn't been kidding. Addy was wet, totally slick for him. Her supple thighs felt like silk and had tone. Gripping her to keep her open, he sought the taut pearl he'd sucked not long ago. Her clit was full, and he licked and teethed her into a writhing mess.

He loved it. She tasted like his woman, her scent going straight to his head. He wanted to come inside her, to fill her up. But he'd done that once. In her mouth too. He had yet to take her ass. From what she'd said, she hadn't had anal sex in a while. But the sparkle in her eye when he'd mentioned it showed him she had a few kinks they had yet to discover.

He couldn't wait. He ate her out, loving her breathy moans and pleas for satisfaction. He ran his hands between her thighs, then inserted a finger in her pussy while he licked her.

"Yes, Noel. Baby, I'm coming."

He wanted to feel her over his lips, and he licked her faster, driving his tongue into her snug body while he savored the taste of her.

She cried out and came, and he continued to enjoy her, loving the sweet cream gathering just for him. He could have risen over her and shoved deep, coming with her. So attuned to her pleasure, he wanted it all around him. But she had to want it all, and he needed her to be ready.

He petted her to calm her down, running his hands over the strip of hair covering her sex, over the slick folds guarding her secrets. Her taut belly and full breasts heaved as she caught her breath.

"Noel. My God."

He chuckled and kissed his way up her body, resting at her nipple. "And we're just getting started."

"I came so hard."

"I know. So tasty." He licked his lips, her slack face so pretty, so fine. She parted her lips and he had to know her again.

He rose and kissed her, taken with the way she loved his mouth. No easy pecks or simple kisses for Addy. She made love to his lips and tongue, her every touch one of care, of sensual gratitude.

He felt her small hands run down his belly then cup his balls. He arched into her touch and deepened the kiss, trembling with the need to be inside her.

"You're so hot. So strong." She ran a hand up his forearm to curl around his biceps, while the other tortured him by stroking his cock and balls until he found himself rocking into her hand, unable to stop. "I love feeling you come in me."

"Shit, Addy." He hated to swear around a woman, but Addy destroyed him. "I mean, stop. I don't want to come on your belly. I want inside your ass."

She rolled his balls, and he closed his eyes and stilled.

"I want that too." She let him go, and he opened his eyes and watched her watching him.

She turned onto her belly and tilted her ass up. "In me, right?"

"Gently," he promised, hoping he didn't look as desperate as he felt. He reached into the drawer next to the bed and withdrew the lube. He drizzled it over his cock, then parted her cheeks and gave her some. "I want you nice and slick," he said.

Noel blanketed her, resting his cock along the seam in her ass.

"You feel heavy. You have a big dick, Noel. Can I take you?" she asked in a tone that completely did him in.

"Are you trying to make me come before I'm in you?"

She laughed, a seductress's weapon wielded with precision. Then she arched up again, sliding his cock against her. "We wouldn't want that."

Where had this woman come from? This was no innocent schoolteacher or friendly neighbor. She owned him with a smile, a dark look, a seductive laugh.

He edged against her, slowly dragging along her crease, trying to stimulate the more superficial nerve endings. Then he couldn't take any more of her moans and silken feel. He angled his cock at her hole and gave a small push.

She tensed, and he stopped, sweating, wanting nothing more than to shove home.

"*Oh.*"

He remained motionless. It was Addy impaling herself on his cock as she slowly rocked back into him while he balanced on his hands above her.

"More?" he asked, his voice gritty.

"Yes. You don't hurt." She sounded surprised.

"It's not as bad if you go slow and you're lubed." Most people thought anal sex to be painful, that it needed preparation. It did, but not so much that a woman needed to walk around with a dildo up her ass for days to take a dick.

He wanted to smile at the mental image, but he had no humor left, not with desire riding him so hard.

Noel gave her a little bit more, let her get used to him, then pulled out and pushed back in. Slow increments, until Addy was right there with him, needing the whole of his length.

When Noel seated himself all the way, he closed his eyes and saw stars, enraptured with such closeness.

"Addy, Addy," he continued to chant. "So good, baby."

"Move in me," she ordered and pushed back once more.

"Easy." If she did that again, he'd ram too deep, because he was barely hanging on to his control.

"Does it feel good? Because it feels good to me." Again she sounded surprised.

"Told you you'd beg me."

She laughed and moaned. "I bet you're close to begging *me*."

"You have no idea," he said through gritted teeth as he withdrew a fraction, only to slide back inside such a tight, hot grip. "Oh Addy. I need to move. Need to fuck you. So much."

"Do it, baby. Give it to me."

He did his best to be careful, but he feared he was moving too fast too soon.

Then Addy yelled for him to move faster. Harder.

And Noel lost it.

So close, on the edge, and he pumped hard twice more and seized in a wave of bliss so extreme he was frozen. He could have been stabbed, shot, hung, threatened with a flame thrower, and he'd have been unable to respond, in thrall as he emptied into Addy's perfect, amazing ass.

It took him some time to come back to himself, and he ended by moving in and out of her in tiny motions, until his sensitivity became too much.

He finally withdrew and slumped over her, kissing her shoulders and neck. "Addy, I can't move." He sank into her until she grumbled about his weight.

He withdrew and grudgingly left the bed to clean himself. He came back to help clean her as well, then snuggled in bed with her.

"Okay, honey?" He cradled her head on his chest, stroking her back, and knew he'd finally come home.

"It was…"

Her pause alarmed him, and he sat up in a hurry. "What? I didn't hurt you, did I?"

Her angelic smile had his heart racing even faster. She was it for him. He knew it. But it was all so sudden, wasn't it?

"It was *amazing*. You're amazing. You and that big, thick, tasty penis."

He cringed. "You had me until 'penis.' A little too clinical."

She sighed. "Sorry. I got carried away. How about thick, tasty cock?"

"Much better." He wanted to get back to being tasty, just as soon as he got a bit of rest. "Addy?"

"Hmm?"

"I swear I'll be ready for round two soon. I just need a minute to enjoy my post-coital bliss."

"Now that's a mouthful." They both paused. "I made it too easy, didn't I?" Addy groaned.

"You did. But we'll get back to that mouthful comment soon enough." He chuckled. She joined him, and the laughter settled them both into a companionable rest.

ADDY HAD NEVER IMAGINED sex could be so much fun, or so satisfying. Even the positions that she thought should have hurt or been awkward felt natural with Noel. He was the one she wanted. The one she'd waited for.

She hoped she wasn't confusing exceptional sex for emotional closeness, but heaven help her, Noel had given her multiple orgasms. Sex with him was liberating and fun, because he took the time to pay attention to her needs. So giving, so sincere.

So deadly.

She studied his body, aware he had more bruises than he'd had Saturday. Perhaps he'd gotten hurt during the fight in Seattle. But he didn't act injured at all. He sure the heck hadn't moved as if he had pain.

She cuddled closer to him, wishing every night could be spent in his arms. Every day spent waking up heartbeat to heartbeat. She toyed with the sleek chest under her, wondering if he naturally had little hair or if he shaved. Either way, she loved his body. So hard and muscular.

Noel had seemed underwhelming at first glance. Handsome and cold without the appearance of physical toughness. But without his clothes on, the man had a solid framework. Solid. A terrific word to describe Noel.

"I'm quitting the business, Addy."

"So you said." She tried not to be too hopeful about that.

"I mean it. And this just… I want to be with you. I want to be a man you can respect."

She heard the buried question in his words and leaned up to see his face. "I do respect you, Noel. You're a good man."

"Who does bad things." He sighed. "I want to be a good man who does good things. No more lies. No more tearing things down. I want to build a life." He ran his hands through her hair and cupped her cheek. "I want to build it with you, Addy."

She smiled down at him, feeling tenderness for the man still so guarded. His emotions for her seemed so obvious, but he hadn't come out and said he loved her. Yet building a life with someone meant trust. He'd trusted her enough to tell her the truth, hadn't he?

"For all that we've known each other, we haven't really *known* each other until recently."

He stroked her hair once more and nodded.

"So I hope I don't seem crazy when I say I love you, Noel."

He stopped. "What?"

She caressed his chest, feeling his heart race like crazy. "I love you. That toughness, that sarcastic wit. The way you move, the power in your body and soul. You're a protector more than a killer." She paused. "Do you enjoy ending life?"

"Is it wrong if I say sometimes?"

"But the people you end, they do bad things?"

His shadowed expression told her more than words could say. "Yes."

"I know, because I know you. I really do, you know. I might just be an elementary school teacher, not as well-traveled or sophisticated as you. But I know people. And I know I love you."

He pulled her down for a kiss and a hug that lasted a good, long while. "God, I'm so happy right now."

But he hadn't said he loved her.

"And?"

He must have heard a warning in her voice, because he looked up at her, wary, when she pulled back. "And I hope you're happy too?"

She slapped his chest, not hard, but firmly.

"Hey."

"Noel, do you love me?"

He actually sputtered and blushed, and she stared at her answer, surprised she had to ask. "I, well, Addy, I want you to move in with me. I want to marry you. I've been infatuated with you for years."

"But do you love me?" she asked softly, aware she'd startled him. She, boring old Adeline Rose, school teacher, terrified her assassin.

"What I feel for you goes beyond love, and it scares the crap out of me because of the danger we're facing. I don't want to lose you, Addy." He gripped her hand in his, so she could only prop herself on one arm and his chest.

"You love me."

"Yes, yes. I love you." He blew out a breath. "Now with any luck I haven't jinxed us. I haven't had a lot of softness in my life. Not a lot of experience with love. But I don't like being away from you. And don't tell the guys, but Noel Jr. has really grown on me." He blinked away suspicious moisture. "Addy, I imagine a life with you that's so far beyond what I deserve."

"What you *think* you deserve," she corrected, doing her best not to cry with him. "I know I deserve it. I've been good, darn it." She laughed with him. "I love you, Noel. And if you're sure about staying here, I want us to be together. We'll take it slowly, once you're here for sure. I don't want you to have regrets."

He snorted. "That's my line. You can do much better than me. I'm scared once the novelty of having me around wears off, you'll find out I'm too boring for you."

She leaned down to kiss his chest. "Now, Noel. You've met my dad and seen his gardens. Who do you think he passed all that secret gardening information down to? You want big tomatoes and cucumbers like Bert Rose? You have to get them from me."

"So you're saying that in order to learn how to grow like a pro, I have to seduce my neighbor? That's more Deacon's style. I'm more of a fixer. But..." He smiled and kissed her. "I can do it. Maybe if I had more practice though."

In a slick move, he had her on her back, his hand in the

drawer fishing out a condom. "Let's put this on and try again. I'm not sure I have the hang of missionary. And being old and boring, I should really know how to do this one position, shouldn't I?"

Ready to take him on once more, she wrapped her legs around his waist and nodded. "Yes, you should. Then I'll tutor you in math, and we'll take a closer look at the number sixty-nine."

He groaned on a laugh and entered her, and then there was no more talk as they both became the teacher, and the student, in bed.

TWO DAYS LATER, Noel was still on cloud nine. Yes, he now owed Hammer for disposing of two bodies—and not in his garden, thank you very much. Yes, they were no closer to determining the father of Noel Jr. since the lab had gotten the results screwed up and had to test again, adding more time to the delayed progress. And yes, he was stuck with Deacon and Hammer through it all, because they had decided to stay to help stop the hitmen after Noel and now Addy and the baby. But life couldn't feel any more perfect.

Deacon and Hammer actually liked the little guy, though Hammer did his best not to touch the baby, afraid of hurting him. Deacon had no problem toting the kid along, because it helped him pick up chicks—his words.

Solene grudgingly stayed at Addy's while Addy stayed

with Noel. Solene would soon go back to her house, and when she did, he knew Deacon or Hammer planned to go with her. At least until they worked out who had targeted them. Solene would be in danger on her own.

They'd upped security at her daycare, at Addy's school and in her classroom, though the ladies remained unaware of Noel's extra precautions, because he didn't trust the quiet.

The men he'd killed—*in his own fucking house*—were the key to the puzzle he was slowly trying to work out. Hammer hadn't gotten very far, though he had learned a vital clue in Pennsylvania.

Someone wanted all three of them dead for a purported wrong they'd done him on a job overseas.

That meant Noel, Deacon, and Hammer had all been involved in a particular mission. It wasn't just Noel, as Deacon had already confirmed. Hearing Hammer say the same made it certain. That made Noel feel better about ordering the guys to stay. Not just for the baby, but to clear up potential danger. It was bad enough they had to watch their backs during regular civilian life. But to be in the middle of an op with an extra target painted on their backs? No way.

The phone rang while he stood in his greenhouse and spliced a new tomato plant he wanted to try. "Noel here," he answered.

"Noel, it's Addy."

"Hey, beautiful."

"I wanted to remind you we had an early day today because we're prepping for teacher conferences." She paused. "I'm going to finish up here then head to lunch with Brent."

He put down his clippers. "What's that?"

She sighed. "Brent called me yesterday. We've been friends for years. We've dated a bit, but we've never been serious. At least, not on my end. He was hoping for something else. I think I owe it to him to tell him face to face I'm seeing someone else."

"You mean, that you love someone else, and he could never be more than a pale substitute for my manliness."

"Yes, something like that," she said dryly.

He nodded, pleased. "Just let me know where you're going, okay? Somewhere public is good. I'll have Deacon shadow you."

She groaned. "Really? This will be hard enough without knowing I have an audience."

"I could be there instead. You'll never see me. Don't worry."

"I don't know…"

"Addy, it's necessary," he said softly. "I know this is a huge pain, and it's intrusive, but until we know who and why they're after us—all of us, you included—you're in danger."

A small silence. "I'm scared, Noel. When we're together, none of this seems real. But I remember what happened. Before. I-I don't want that to happen again. I worry for you. And I sure don't want anyone I know caught up in it. You think I should just tell Brent over the phone that we're done?"

"No." As much as he didn't like the thought of her with another man, she needed to feel at least a measure of normalcy in her hometown. The people on their tail didn't want the police involved. Only in private would there be more danger. "Just let me know where you're going and I'll be there. Don't worry, honey. You're safe as long as you're in public."

"Okay. I was thinking he and I would go to the Treehouse Café for lunch. We'll be there around two-ish. I'm almost done here at school, then I'm going to stop by Solene's to drop off a sweater she leant me. Brent works nearby, so we'll meet up at the daycare before driving to Treehouse together. Then you can drive me back to my car, okay?"

"You need to go together?" He didn't like that.

"It's our thing. We're friends, and that's kind of what we do."

"Fine." He made a few notes. "I'll see you at two. Text me if you have any problems. Anything at all."

"I will. I love you."

He felt warm all over. "I love you too, Addy."

She hung up and he went back to his garden. He had a feeling he'd have the biggest and best crop this year with all the positive energy he'd been feeling.

AN HOUR LATER, Deacon and Hammer found him typing in the basement on the secured server. Noel thought he might have found someone else to add to their list.

"Noel, you need to see something." Deacon sounded grim.

Behind him, Hammer nodded.

"What's up?" He followed the pair upstairs to Deacon's laptop. The television showed a soccer game, muted in the background.

"This." Deacon turned the laptop to show the feed from Addy's school. "You see that guy?"

Noel peered at one of the maintenance men. "That logo…"

"Yeah." Hammer nodded. "Same red letters, same logo as the one Bob was wearing. You remember Bob? The dead guy whose neck you snapped?"

"Hell." Noel was already getting his keys when Deacon swore. "What now?"

"There's someone at Solene's who's been bothering me. A new handyman she's been dealing with. Says his name is

Franks. Weird thing is I found a buried set of prints under the Franks name. His other prints come up Jon Wilkes."

Noel felt panic when he should have been ice-cold. "Deacon, you go to Solene's. Hammer, you stay here with the baby. You can feed us intel while protecting him. I'll pick up Addy at the school."

"She's not there," Hammer said. "She left ten minutes ago. Best bet, head to Solene's and meet her there."

"Let's go, guys. I have a feeling all hell's about to break loose."

THIRTEEN

Addy pulled into the parking lot and saw Solene's car there. The daycare had closed early the day before due to some maintenance issues—there seemed to be a lot of bad pipes on the island lately. Solene had not been happy. She'd ripped her handyman a new one. Even Deacon had felt for the guy, or so he'd continually said.

Addy smiled, loving the fact Solene had met two men she couldn't wrap around her little finger. Three, including Noel, but he was taken. Deacon and Hammer seemed to see through Solene's beauty, neither man giving in to the termagant's demands. They didn't seem intimidated by her either, which Addy also loved.

Solene had no problem with Hammer. They seemed to treat each other like tolerable siblings, and spending so much time together, that was a good thing. But Deacon… He and Solene were like oil and water. But Addy had a feeling with a little time, they might actually strike sparks off each other that would explode into flame. Problem was,

Deacon wasn't the settling type, and Solene still hated men in general—just Hammer and Noel a little less.

And then there was that pesky target hanging over the group of them.

She sighed and parked the car. Before exiting, she glanced around. Seeing the lot mostly empty except for locals moving around to neighboring stores and buildings, she felt safe enough to leave the car. She hurried inside, fingering the earrings Noel claimed were his favorite. The dangly loops made her feel pretty, and since he'd actually had an opinion about them, she'd worn them to make him happy.

Once inside the daycare she heard Solene arguing in the back. No one else was in, apparently, because the place appeared spotless and kid-free.

Until that plumbing issue was fixed, it figured the daycare would have to be closed. Addy felt Solene's pain. That issue with the bathroom at school had unnerved her. Fortunately, they had a decent maintenance crew and had fixed the problem quickly. The pipe problem had also given her an opportunity to introduce the children to the concept of plumbing. So a win-win, despite the potential mess.

"Solene," she called out. "It's just me."

"I'll be right out," Solene growled from the back. "You're kidding me! I already talked to Ralph, and his estimate... *What?*" A low murmur answered her.

Addy pitied the handyman. A new guy in town, he'd been

highly recommended by the accountant and massage therapists next door. Even Brent had used him once a few months ago.

And speaking of which… Addy waited for Brent to arrive, nervous about letting him down. Though they hadn't hit it off exactly, they'd always been friendly. She had a difficult time understanding why he thought they could move beyond being just friends, though. She felt no chemistry with him at all, though he had decent enough looks and personality.

He had never acted super attracted to her either. Not like Noel did.

She flushed, remembering how he'd woken her this morning…right before having to hustle out of bed to deal with a fussy baby.

Addy smiled.

After a while, she didn't hear anything in the back. Strange.

The door jangled. She looked over her shoulder to see Brent.

He waved. "Hey. Ready to go?"

"Sure. Just let me check on Solene first."

"No problem." Brent ran his own business, so precluding any client meetings, he never had any issues with time.

Addy walked into the back and sought the break room,

where she expected to find Solene. Except she didn't. Addy froze.

Tied up and gagged, lying on the ground, were two of Solene's employees, Marge and Annie. Tears streaked down their faces and they looked beyond scared.

Addy hurried to pull her phone out of her purse and call Noel when a hand knocked it away and someone yanked her by the hair out of the room.

"*Ow.* Stop it!" She hoped Brent heard her. "Let me go! What are you doing? Where is Solene?" she yelled and gripped her bag tightly.

The grip on her hair ceased, and she turned around. But when she spotted the intruder, she froze. Terror filled her. The man from the restaurant in Seattle, the one Noel hadn't killed, stared at her with evil glee.

"Well, well, the pretty bitch I never got to play with. Been spreading your legs for Ice, huh? Who knew the prick had it in him?" The man laughed, an ugly, wheezing sound, made uglier by the cruelty in his face. "Your fuckbuddy killed my brother. Now I'm gonna kill his whore."

Addy couldn't move. "W-where's Solene?"

"The blonde piece of ass with the mouth that never quits?" He snorted, and she realized he was wearing the same type of maintenance shirt the handyman had sported. He moved with a severe limp that had to be hurting like the devil. "She's tied up in the back. We're saving her for something special."

We're saving her. More than just him, then. Addy threw off her panic enough to shout, "Brent, run! They have guns. Call the police!" just as Deacon burst through the back door and knocked the man away.

Addy ran down the hallway, needing to find Solene. Instead, she encountered two more maintenance men holding knives, walking toward her. Feeling silly for not remembering it sooner, she dug into her purse, pulled out a Taser, and tagged one of the men.

He went down seizing, and she threw her bag at the other while yelling for Solene.

"Addy? I called the police…" Brent entered into the hallway and pulled her behind him just as the other man reached them. Then Brent shocked her by decking the guy.

Deacon popped out of the room. "Solene?"

"Another one?" Brent looked as if he planned to move toward Deacon.

"Wait, Brent. He's a friend." She was breathing hard, looking over Brent's shoulder. "I don't know. Down the hall?"

Deacon shoved the man Brent had hit back down. Then he snapped the man's arm and kneed him in the chest, causing him to shriek in pain and remain down. Deacon kicked the knife away and disappeared down the hall. She heard muffled shots she knew came from a silenced gun.

She and Brent stared at each other.

"Who was that?" he asked. "What the *hell* is going on?"

"It's a long story."

Understandably, he seemed a little wild around the eyes. "Let's get out of here."

She nodded, and they hurried out of the daycare, into his nearby business a few doors down. They sat, stunned.

"Ah, police should be here soon," he said.

"Good. Thanks." She refused to cry. Noel would want her to be strong. She knew she should call him, but she'd left her phone behind.

"So much for lunch." Brent rubbed his stomach. "Is it weird I'm still hungry?"

They both laughed, she a little hysterically. His cell phone buzzed.

"Oh, when you're done with that, can I make a call?" she asked.

"Sure." He nodded and answered it. "This is Brent Morgan." He watched her while he talked, and she thought he'd taken the incident much better than she had. "Yes. It's all working out. We're good. Thanks. You've been a big help. Make sure we don't leave any threads behind. Sloppy work won't get the job done."

Brent smiled and disconnected, then handed the phone to her. "Here you go."

She dialed Noel's number.

"Who is this?"

"Noel, it's me. It's Addy."

She felt his sigh through the phone. "Thank God. Where are you?"

"I'm in Brent's office down from Solene's daycare. Deacon's in there. There were people with guns and knives. I saw the man from Seattle. He..." She glanced at Brent, saw his encouraging nod. "He had some of Solene's workers tied up. I couldn't find Solene, but Deacon went after her. Noel, there were men there in maintenance uniforms. The guy from Seattle was dressed like Solene's handyman."

"We know. Look, sit tight. Can I talk to Brent?"

"Sure. He called the police, they should be here soon."

Brent took the phone. "Hello?"

"Brent, this is Noel. Addy's friend. Look, can you guys just sit tight? I'll be there in five minutes. We have a situation, and I'll explain it when I get there."

"Oh, don't worry, Ice. Addy and I are good friends. Don't you worry about anything. I'll make sure she's safe and sound. You get your little friends together. Make sure Shadow and Destroyer take care of the cleanup. Wouldn't want to involve the locals, now would we?"

Addy frowned. "What—?"

Brent held up a finger to stop her from talking. "Now

we've got things to do. See you soon, loverboy." Brent hung up and pocketed his phone. Then he grabbed his keys. "Well? Come on, Addy."

She blinked. "What was all that about?" She had a very bad feeling about Brent, especially seeing the cold, yet satisfied look on his face. She backed up a step and stopped when he invaded her space and put a hand at her throat. The sure suddenness shocked her. As did the notion she didn't know this man at all.

"Uh-uh. Come on, Addy. We're friends, remember? Time to go to lunch so we can talk about our future." He grabbed her by the arm and jerked her with him out the back, where a dark blue sedan waited. She'd never seen this vehicle before.

"Let me go, Brent, if that's even your name."

He laughed. "Aren't you smart? Did Ice fill you in on a contractor's life? When he was humping that pretty pussy, did he spill the beans?"

She cringed.

"Don't worry. He can have you. You're not my type. I don't take leavings from the minor leagues, anyway. I'm a top tier kind of a guy. I only sleep with angels." He found that hilarious and laughed as he shoved her toward the trunk of the car. He opened it and tossed her inside. She banged her head, hard, and tried to focus her vision when the trunk slammed shut, locking her in.

Terrified, she cried, praying Noel would find her in time.

Because Brent looked exactly like a killer, no softness or vulnerability in his gaze. No, he looked like a psychopath. Nothing like her assassin with a heart of gold.

She could only hope she wouldn't be the weakness that got Noel killed, because Brent had every intention of stringing out his torture. She could feel it.

NOEL'S WORST NIGHTMARE, that Addy would be dragged kicking and screaming into his world and be hurt because of him, had suddenly come true.

Brent Morgan. How the fuck had he missed Brent being in on everything? The man had checked out from the get-go. Noel had to concentrate, because the images of her being tormented haunted him. He called Hammer.

"Yo."

"Brent Morgan, Addy's friend. He's our guy." He described the call. "He has to be Business. Either a handler or contractor. He knew all our codenames. And he's got Addy."

"Shit. Look, Deacon has the daycare handled. Solene's good. I got the baby, and I'm ready for bear. Go get her. I'll look into this Morgan guy."

Noel parked on the side of the road, no longer in a hurry to reach Solene. He pulled up the tracker app he'd used on Addy. The small tag on her earrings, a precaution in case she lost her phone. Since hers appeared in the daycare and she'd called from Brent's cell, he couldn't count on her phone's location.

But her earrings told another story. He followed them as they continued to move away from town, into what felt like the middle of nowhere. He drove faster, determined to save his woman. Or die trying.

As he drove and the minutes ticked away, he continued to coordinate with Hammer. Brent Morgan was thirty-five. An accountant and financial advisor who'd moved to the island three years ago. He kept a low profile, did some traveling because he apparently had a house in the Cayman Islands, money inherited from his deceased parents, but otherwise flew under the radar. Nothing he didn't already know.

What was the motive? He didn't recognize the picture Hammer had sent him, nor did the man's name come up through Big Joe's connections. Angel. X6TFL. Brent Morgan. What the heck was the connection? Not Mexico… Or could it have been the Sinaloa job? But that made no sense. They'd rid the world of drug runners and sex slavers. None of the Business had been in on it except Deacon and Hammer, with Noel offering peripheral backup at best.

Unless Deacon and Hammer weren't on the up and up?

No. They had solid alibis, for one. And two, he knew those men. They might be a pain in the ass, but they weren't traitors or villains.

"He's deep in the woods," Hammer said through the car speaker. "Near a house registered under another name," Hammer said. "Oh, and Deacon's on his way."

"Solene's good then?"

"She's pissed as hell. Just fine. The cops arrived. No idea how we're going to spin this."

"We'll worry about it later. I have to save Addy."

"Yeah, you do." With Hammer's help, they triangulated Addy's position.

Noel pulled into the area a half mile down the road. He took out a pack, filled with the supplies he'd need and that he kept in a hidden compartment in his car at all times. Then he set off with his phone on, his headset in his ear, ready to explode into action and deal with Brent once and for all.

ADDY SAT in the chair and didn't move. With a gun trained on her, and with no urge to have half her face blown off, she ignored her bladder and remained motion-less. The run-down but cozily furnished cabin in the isolated woods would have been an ideal retreat under other circumstances.

Across from her, sitting in a plush chair with his legs crossed, Brent braced his elbow on the arm of the chair and kept his small pistol aimed at her.

"So, um, are you going to tell me why?"

He shrugged. "Why what?"

"Why did you do this? Why be my friend for years if you didn't even like me?"

"Honey, I like you." She hated hearing him call her "honey." When Noel did it she felt loved. Right now, she felt revolted. "You're bait, plain and simple."

"I thought we were friends."

"*Were?* Addy, we *are* friends." Brent's smile looked more than off. That lack of expression in his eyes made him seem creepy. Serial killer-like.

"Then why all this? Why the baby? Why try to kill Noel?"

"Let me tell you a story."

Finally. Some answers. She just hoped she'd be alive to tell Noel.

"A long time ago a boy was living in the streets, trying to stay away from his drug-addled mother and all her boyfriends who liked to visit—who liked to play with her children, the younger the better.

"This boy was smart. He knew his sisters and baby brother would distract her boyfriends while he did his best to get rid of them. So he used his siblings as bait, and while Mom's boyfriends got busy, he slit their throats." He paused to glance down at his phone. "He made a good bit of money, because Mom was pretty and her babies were beautiful. Neurotic, seriously screwed-up by this point, but so pretty."

Brent smiled, and she saw a hint of that beauty under the cruel man. "It's a harsh tale. Nothing like the little angels in your classrooms."

"I'm sorry, Brent."

He shrugged. "Life isn't always pretty. The story has a good ending. The boy was so good at his job, he grabbed the attention of a local gang. He played them all, taking over the neighborhood. And that attracted even better attention. A program not acknowledged by the government yet does government work. They legitimize murder and violence, all to help America stay beautiful." He smiled. "I went to work. I did better and better. I rose up the ranks. And I scored Big Joe as my handler."

He sat up, lowering the gun. "Did you know he works with all your friends? Ice, Shadow, and Destroyer?"

From the names, she gathered who they were. Ice was obviously Noel. Shadow, Deacon. And Destroyer had to be Hammer.

"Big Joe's a big wig in the organization. I think he might be the owner, but no one can say for certain who really bankrolls what we do." He rubbed the gun against his leg. "Or I should say, what we *did*."

He stared at her. "You know you'll never be able to tell Noel this. If he even makes it this far to the cabin." An explosion outside punctured his words, and he gave her a big grin. "Yes, he's out there. Wonder if he can make it through my maze? Anyway, if your lover makes it this far, I'll shoot you. And it will hurt, Addy. So much." He tsked. "Like they hurt Angel."

"Who is Angel?" Hadn't Noel mentioned her name on one side of the baby's locket?

"A good friend of mine. I loved her. I hated her. But I didn't kill her. Oh sure, I wanted to. But she disappeared, and then Big Joe had her taken out. But he had help."

He just watched her.

"You think Noel and the others did it?"

"I don't know. I think they might have."

"But why are you doing this to them? You're the one hunting Noel down. The one who sent all those men to try to kill him?"

"It's fun, and he really needs to keep on his toes. He's taken to relaxing on the island a little too much. A contractor has to be sharp, Addy. Noel's not doing too badly though. He took out my men in Seattle when he landed. Then he destroyed the ones sent to take you last week. And just a few days ago, he killed my other team. Of course, they were all amateurs, but still, Noel isn't doing half bad. Sloppy though. He should never have left you all by yourself."

"He didn't."

"But he did. He was too slow, not where he needed to be."

Another explosion outside. Brent checked his phone and frowned. "He's getting closer."

Addy started crying. "Brent, let me go. I'm not part of this." And if she got free, she'd find a way to warn Noel away, to keep him safe, somehow.

"Shh. Don't cry." Brent brought her a tissue and dried her tears. Then he stepped back and aimed the gun at her.

"Brent?"

"We all have a part to play, Adeline. Now play yours."

He fired, and the ice in her leg turned to a conflagration of pain that had her crying out despite her effort to not give Brent the satisfaction.

"That's just a love tap," he chided. "Let's try again."

This time he aimed higher, at her midsection. Addy lunged out of the chair, needing to protect herself.

Another explosion, this one so close it rocked the house.

But it didn't stop Brent from firing. And it didn't stop the pain from dragging her down, down, into the dark.

FOURTEEN

N oel didn't have much time. He knew that. But Deacon's help made all the difference. While Deacon set off the many traps in the woods, Noel had made a beeline for the cabin.

He'd left Deacon his pack and only had his Jericho to take care of Brent Morgan, a man who still didn't seem to exist. Noel had left his phone with Deacon, on the off chance Brent had a way to keep track of it.

But that put him out of communication. He had no idea what he'd be getting into.

He approached the cabin and belly-crawled the short open distance between the tree line and the side of the home. He saw a side window, presumably leading to a basement.

Hammer hadn't found any layouts of the place, but he'd cautioned Noel to be wary of booby-traps and alarms.

Noel thought he could squeeze through the window, but

the wires there told him he had to forego it. So he set an explosive at the window and moved on. He carefully did a perimeter run of the house, alert for any sign of trouble. Nothing. Listening close, he heard a low voice. He drew closer to the underside of a window, where a small hole afforded him a better view.

Glancing through the decrepit wall, he saw Addy siting in a chair, Brent Morgan across from her holding a gun.

He listened while the bastard explained himself. None of it made any sense. Angel and Brent? A prodigy of Big Joe? None of the guys had anything to do with Angel's demise.

That we know of.

Had Big Joe used them to dispose of her without them knowing? And if so, what did that mean for the baby or Angel? Was she actually dead, then?

To his horror, Brent stood over Addy and drew his gun. *Move, Addy. Get out of there!*

"We all have a part to play, Adeline. Now play yours," Brent said, then fired.

Noel hit the trigger on the bomb, counted down the three-second delay…

"That's just a love tap. Let's try again."

Addy moved just as the bomb blew. Noel straightened and fired through the window, careful not to catch Addy in the crossfire. But the bastard must have been expecting him as he dove out of sight. Noel rocketed through the glass, catching himself on the jagged edges. The pain didn't matter. Addy lying on the ground, bleeding, unmoving, mattered.

He became Ice because he had to. He felt a bullet tear through his side as he launched himself at Brent. They fought for the gun. Brent was good, but Ice was better. Noel disarmed him and tossed the gun to the ground.

Brent drew a knife from his back holster and lunged. Noel fought back, taking a few slices to his arm and hand but not allowing himself to feel anything.

He funneled all his rage, his pain, at Brent. He ducked a vicious jab aimed at his throat and rammed his head up, hitting Brent under the chin.

The bastard was off balance and shaky now, and Noel ignored a feeling of dizziness and tackled him to the ground. They rolled for dominance while Noel continued to hit Brent in the ribs, the gut, the groin, any soft part he took pleasure in annihilating, until he heard Brent wheeze and knew he'd broken a few ribs and possibly punctured a lung.

Noel found the knife lying on the ground by Brent's side. He gripped it and shoved the blade into Brent's belly, staring down the fucker who'd tried to kill all he held dear. "Go to hell."

Blood bubbled on Brent's lips. "Been there."

Noel twisted the knife. He saw Brent's frown, then a delighted smile that didn't belong there.

Too late, he registered another person in the room and heard the gunshot. But he didn't feel any pain. He rolled off Brent and saw a dark-haired woman clutching her throat and gasping as she fell to her knees. A gun tumbled out of her hands.

Addy lay on her side, Brent's gun outstretched in her hands. She saw Noel staring at her and gave him a pained smile. "Could have told you I'm a crack shot." Then she collapsed in on herself and moaned, "I'm okay. I'm alive. You're good. We're good." She continued to mutter, conscious, in pain, but she'd be okay, he prayed.

Brent whispered something.

Noel reluctantly turned back to him, needing any kind of information he could get before the bastard died.

"What?"

Brent whispered, "Nine. I'm really…" Unintelligible words. "…nine. Angel man. Coming."

Then he died.

Deacon shouted, "I'm coming in. Are we clear?"

"In here," Noel shouted back and tried to stand, to cross to Addy. But he couldn't make his legs work. That should have bothered him, the ice creeping up his body. It didn't. It was just one more obstacle to overcome before he reached the love of his life.

Deacon entered and took in the scene just as Noel managed to crawl to her.

"Addy, baby. You okay?" She'd been shot in the leg. Not a bad wound. Especially because it appeared to have grazed her, not near a vital artery. But the gut wound worried him.

"I hurt." She reached for and found his blood-covered hand. "You look terrible," she said, blinking up at him.

"I've been better," he admitted, letting the ice sweep over him. "So sorry, Addy. Love you...so...much." He felt himself falling. "Don't leave," he wanted to add *me*, but his mouth wasn't working anymore. He could no longer feel her hands, but he could sense her near.

And that was enough, that she lived and was loved. By him.

"IT WAS A FUCKING NIGHTMARE, that's what it was," Noel heard as he woke, feeling groggy and undone by all the sunlight filtering into...his bedroom?

"Oh, look. Mr. Lazy is finally up and awake. Jesus, Noel. Take a vacation why don't you?"

He blinked and focused. Deacon had the baby in his arms, swinging the kid around in an unsafe manner while the baby laughed. Solene frowned at him but didn't say anything. She had a few bruises on her face, but being Solene, she managed to make them look fashionable.

Hammer stood behind Addy, watching Noel with a mix of worry and relief. "Finally. Took you four damn days."

An IV and monitor sat next to his bed. An unfamiliar woman fluttered around him wearing jeans and a T-shirt. He instinctively reached for his gun and swore when he jerked his arm too fast.

"Easy. She's good," Hammer said with a grin. "I vetted her myself."

"Pain in my ass," the young woman grumbled. "Why the hell would Big Joe send someone unsuitable?"

"Her name is Violet. She goes by Vi," Addy said.

"And she can talk too," Vi said as she bustled out of the room.

He turned and drank her in. "You look wonderful," he said, his voice scratchy. Addy had a bruised cheekbone. She wore a robe over pajama pants. He imagined she'd been bandaged up around her abdomen and leg. "Damage?"

"Shh. Don't talk." She fed him an ice chip that tasted better than anything he'd had in years. "I'm fine. My leg hurts, but it's healing. It was just a scratch, apparently." She glared at Hammer.

"Hey, you wanted the truth. For all that whining, you were barely touched."

She turned her angry green eyes back on him and her expression eased. God, he loved her so much. "Yes, well, it hurt. I've never been shot before."

"Trust me, it's not fun," Vi muttered as she returned briefly to remove some bloody bandages from the room.

"Your belly?" Noel asked, needing to know. To see and touch her.

"Easy." Hammer and Addy gently pushed him back down. "She's fine," Hammer said. "Bullet passed through her and didn't hit anything major. A few weeks of rest and she'll be good as new."

Solene drew near, deliberately turning her back on Deacon, who frowned. "That means no sex, you two."

Addy blushed. "Solene. Really. He's barely back."

"Yeah, but he's got that look. No boning, Mr. Ice, or you'll break her stitches," she admonished.

He gave a pained grin, feeling all was right with the world. "No secrets, I see."

To his surprise, Deacon looked uncomfortable. "She had a right to know, considering those assholes tried to pound her into the floor." Then he grinned. "You should have seen her work on them. Solene knows how to move—for a civilian."

She flipped her hair back. "Black belt, buddy. Don't you forget it."

"I'm in love," Deacon teased.

Solene blushed but her glare remained. "Whatever. So Noel, you're apparently retired now. Hammer talked to someone who knows someone, and you're out."

Hammer nodded. "And not on any lists, so you're clean. I

had a talk with Big Joe." He frowned. "But we'll discuss that later.

"No, now." He saw Hammer and Deacon exchange a glance. "Addy, would you and Solene take the baby out? I need to talk to the guys."

She gave him a peck on the cheek and caressed his hair. "Sure thing, sexy." She stood, and Solene took the boy from Deacon. "I love you, Noel."

He smiled back. "I love you too, Addy." He watched her leave, able to put up with any amount of pain for the sight of his woman.

Hammer made a face. "Okay, just stop. I'm hurting watching all this sap."

"Prop me up, would you?" Noel hated being supine, even if he did have a pillow or two under him. "What's my damage?"

Deacon answered. "Blood loss, mostly. You took a bullet that bounced off a rib, a miracle in itself. So you have bruising. Lots of cuts because of that window you dove through. Impressive, Noel. I saw you go through before I had to take on a few guys in hot pursuit. Brent had a squad staged around the outside of the house, but they had orders to wait until you were in. I didn't." He smiled.

Noel sifted through his memories. "Some of what he said made no sense. He was a contractor, I think. One of Big Joe's, he said."

Hammer shook his head. "That's part of the problem. He wasn't. Big Joe told me he's never seen or heard of Brent Morgan under that name or any other alias. Fingerprints don't show him in the system either. This guy was a ghost."

Noel shifted on the pillows, feeling better about being upright even if his belly protested. He glanced down at his forearms to see them all bandaged up. He looked like a mummy, but he didn't care. "Something else he said..." Another thought struck him. "There was a woman there, at the end. Who was she?"

"The chick Addy bulls-eyed? Annette Fusco, expensive informant and a woman with ties around the world? I gotta say, I'm impressed. Addy nailed her right between the eyes." Deacon sounded proud.

"Fusco... That name is familiar."

Hammer nodded. "It should be. We've used her before. The fact that Brent was using her too is telling. He might not be in our system, but I'd bet he was one of us. Big Joe is looking into the other handlers and their off-book missions. This might go deeper than anyone realizes. Shadow ops even we're not supposed to touch."

"Hmm." Noel considered it. "That could be. Maybe Brent did work for one of the others. He had a similar background. No family that would care if he went missing, tough, resourceful. But something he said at the end. I don't know if we're done with all this yet."

Hammer and Deacon frowned.

"He mentioned something about 'nine,' about Angel man coming. But I don't know what it means."

"I don't know either." Deacon shook his head. "But we have time to figure it out. Hammer and I are on leave until this is all cleared up. We'll start plugging in the new info while you heal up."

"And Violet? What about her?"

"I'm keeping an eye on her." Hammer scowled. "I don't trust her, though I have no reason not to. Something about her rubs me wrong."

"Nah, don't worry so much, Noel," Deacon said with a grin. "She bothers Hammer the way Solene bothers me. I think it's a case of deluded women not appreciating a godlike male in their presence when they should."

At that, Hammer's scowl turned into a smile. "You really do have a way with words, Deacon."

"I know."

The pair left after a few more reassurances about their new security arrangements.

Addy returned.

Noel wanted to sleep, but he couldn't. Not yet. When she held his hand, stroking the bandages on his palm, he breathed her in and closed his eyes. And he slept.

TWO WEEKS later

Addy rolled her eyes and ordered Noel to stop annoying Vi —for the tenth time in two days. "You really are the worst patient."

"I need to get back up and training."

She knew he hated being weak. And as much as he said he loved hearing how Addy had shot the Fusco woman and saved his life, he hated that she'd needed to defend herself in the first place. Noel had a bad case of the guilts going on. Ice, apparently, had made a return, hurling cold insults at anyone in the vicinity.

Except for Addy.

For the most part, Addy felt up to snuff. Her leg still ached, but not like it had. And the stitches had come out of her belly yesterday. She experienced tenderness but no lasting pain. An ibuprofen and she was good to go.

She had talked to her parents, who planned to come back for Thanksgiving in another month or so. The children at school missed her, but after hearing that their teacher had been involved in that nightmare where some wacko had shot up the local daycare, they'd sent her cards and get-well wishes galore.

Noel's people had been quick in forging the narrative they wanted in the official reports. Not a whisper of anything other than Brent going off his rocker and shooting up

Solene's daycare had made the news. He'd been off his medication, the poor guy. And the story had turned from a raging violent shoot-up to the plight of those with mental illness who didn't get the help they needed.

Everything and everyone had normalled out. Addy planned to go back to work on Monday, after a relaxing weekend with Noel—if she could get the blasted man to ease up. For someone who'd suffered so much, he sure healed fast.

He'd been up and moving last week, against Vi's recommendation. He'd also pulled some stitches that needed re-stitching. And then she'd seen Vi's temper in action. Not a woman she wanted to piss off, though Hammer had been more than intrigued.

"What do you really think of Vi?" she asked.

"Aside from being a human vampire? Always taking my blood? She's okay, I guess."

"Noel." Addy laughed and sat next to him on the back porch of his home. They watched the others playing a brutal game of badminton in the backyard. Guys against girls. And the guys were getting their butts handed to them. "What's really wrong, baby?"

He gripped her hand. "I'm sorry. I don't mean to be a jerk."

"You just can't help yourself." She smiled to take the sting out.

He laughed. He did that a lot more around her now. The

guys had accused her of melting Ice. And she liked the notion.

"Addy, I'm out now. I'm done with the profession." He seemed uncomfortable. "I don't know what to do with myself, exactly. But I'll find something. I swear."

"I know. It's okay, Noel. You're in no rush. I'm not, at least. We can take it slow. You're smart. You probably have savings. If not, I have some. It's not much on a teacher's salary, but my parents kind of gave me their place rent-free." What a blessing.

His cheeks turned that delightful shade of pink that looked so incongruous on a face that could freeze a man in his tracks. "I'm not poor, you know."

"Of course not." She hoped she hadn't hurt his feelings.

"I mean, I'm *really* not. The Business paid us well. Very, very well. And I know how to invest." He blew out a breath. "I never have to work again if I don't want to."

She stared. "Oh, well… You're rich?"

"Pretty much." He shrugged. "I want to marry you. I want us to live here. And then there's the baby."

She bit back a grin, so happy her joy threatened to burst through her. "Right. The baby. Can we please give him a name now?"

"None of us knows who he belongs to. But I'm ready to make him mine. If the others go back to the life, they can't keep him safe. I can." He looked into her eyes and held her hand. "*We* can."

"Yes." She leaned close to kiss him. "We can. I love you, Noel. And I'll love Griffith too."

"You mean Ryan. Or Daniel. Or maybe Jace, I like that name too." He smiled then sobered. "But Addy, this isn't over. Something you should know…"

"What?"

He leaned closer so the others wouldn't overhear. "I got the DNA results in the mail today."

"Oh my God. And?"

"I didn't wait for the others. I needed to know." He sounded defensive.

"Like I care. Tell me."

He paused. "I'm not going to tell the others yet. I think we should keep this between us, at least for now. We have enough to worry about."

"If you don't tell me, I'm going to give you another scar, *right now.*"

"The father? It's none of us, Addy. *None* of us are the father."

She gaped. "Are you serious?"

"Yes. I'm having a consultant look into this for me discreetly. It's going to take a while, but we're going to see who matches up, DNA-wise, from our organization. Someone sent this boy to me. The name Angel keeps popping up. We have a feeling she was the mother."

He'd told her about this contractor named Angel. A scary woman, but one who must have loved her baby if she'd sent the little guy to Noel.

Addy bit her lip. "Could Brent have been the father?"

"Already checked. No. But that code in the locket means something. Deacon's taken it as his life's mission to find out what." He nodded, seeming satisfied. "Hammer is going to keep looking into Angel. We'll find out what's what and get the baby back to his rightful mother or father. In the meantime, he's ours."

"And if we never find his mother or father?" she asked softly.

"He's ours," he repeated.

She liked that answer, a lot. "That's if we don't have to fight Deacon for him. He's become a little attached." They watched Deacon hurry to put the baby back on the blanket he'd rolled off of. She grinned. "It doesn't help that the baby keeps saying 'Dee-dee.' Deacon is convinced he's trying to say his name." She watched Deacon give Solene a thorough once-over since she was turned the other way. "But you know, Noel, we might not be the only ones fighting to keep him."

"How's that?"

She nodded at Solene. "I could be wrong, but my friend and your friend don't like each other a little *too much*. What if you're not the only one who decides to leave the Business and start a new life on the island?"

"I don't know." He gave Deacon and Solene a thoughtful look. "But I'll bet you fifty bucks it doesn't happen. Deacon is too edgy to settle down. Solene hates men. Ask her. I think you're seeing hearts everywhere because you love me." So smug, her man. "Next thing you'll be telling me Vi and Hammer are a thing." He angled her chin so she could see them arguing over a point. "She's close to braining the giant with her racket."

Vi took being competitive to an all new level.

"Ah, well, maybe not those two. Not yet. But Vi's new. Give her time." She turned back to Noel and kissed him. The heat built, the love between them so strong. "Now how about you and I play hide the gun while the others play their own game?"

"Best idea you've had all week." He darted to his feet as if he'd never been shot.

"Slow down or you'll hurt yourself."

"We need to talk before the fun starts. Come on."

She bit back a groan of disappointment. She and Noel hadn't been intimate since they'd both been shot. "Okay."

He tugged her inside with him and hurried toward his bedroom, then locked them both inside.

"Noel?"

"Math first." He grinned. "Okay, Ms. Rose. Time for numbers. Show me what sixty-nine really means."

She watched him shuck out of his clothes, proudly displaying a scarred up body that never failed to turn her on. With a grin, she slowly took off her own clothes, then laid down on the bed. "Well, Mr. Cavanaugh, first you turn around. And then you…"

It turned out he learned much better by showing, not telling.

FIFTEEN

Deacon watched his friend disappear inside the house with Addy. Lucky bastard.

A shuttlecock beamed him in the head. "Hey." He glanced over at Little Dee, as he'd taken to calling the boy. So cute, that kid. And smart. He babbled a lot, but he seemed like he was taking everything in. Future intelligence man. *That's my kid.*

Deacon felt foolish thinking of the boy as his. The likelihood he'd knocked up a woman and hadn't known it? No way. He was human, but like the others, he was cautious. That and he was almost positive he was sterile. Abuse suffered as a boy had rendered him unable to have children. Or so a doctor had told him in his teens. Considering where he'd come from and the things he'd seen, he hadn't thought that would be a problem.

But seeing Little Dee, watching Ice thaw out and grow to love a woman, it gave a guy thoughts. He glanced at

Solene, wearing her yoga pants and a trendy girly sweat-shirt that did nothing to hide her curves.

Friggin' ex-model. Leave it to Noel to find the perfect woman to mess up Deacon's love life. He had no problem screwing on the move, screwing while not moving, or doing more than one woman at a time. Deacon enjoyed sex in a multitude of ways.

Sex was fun. Lighthearted. Dangerous. Raunchy. But the women never made him want to stick around after. None of them did.

Yet he found himself intrigued by the man-hating Solene Hansen. She had an ass and rack that didn't quit, that was obvious. She also had a face that sure as shit had graced magazine covers and a body that made bikini ads seem indecent.

The moment he'd met her he'd checked her out online. *Damn.* Talk about Ice. She was like a female Noel, but sexy and feminine instead of deadly.

Another shuttlecock beamed him in the head. "Damn it."

"Quit staring at my ass and play, Shaw."

Deacon glared at her. She stuck out her tongue at him.

He grinned. "Is that an invitation?"

"You see?" she said to Vi, the striking nurse and possible Business plant Big Joe had sent to help Noel. "He's impossible."

Vi nodded and held the racket between her knees while she adjusted her long black ponytail. She looked Latina, dark hair, dark skin, dark eyes. She also had a fine figure Hammer couldn't seem to tear his gaze from, and muscle from dealing with the dead-weight of her many patients.

"Try dealing with that giant." She motioned toward Hammer, who tried to look innocent and failed miserably.

"What? What did I do?"

"Please." Vi huffed. "You're constantly rifling through my things, checking on me every five seconds, and I swear I'm missing one of my bras."

Hammer scowled. "Hey now. I'm just making sure you are who you say you are. You got a bra problem, talk to Deacon. He's got the underwear fetish. Not me."

Solene raised a brow. "Is that so?"

Deacon wanted to pound his friend. "Not true." Not exactly. He had a thing for a fine woman in lingerie, and Hammer had seen him checking out an old ad of Solene modeling some lacy stuff.

He'd gotten hard just from an ad in a magazine. Pathetic, and a telling fact he needed to get laid again. Maybe he'd call on Julie from the grocery store. She'd been cute and petite, nice. The total opposite of Solene. And she'd been more than willing.

"If you're missing a bra, try the dryer. Noel's machines eat clothes. I'm missing half of my socks."

"You do laundry?" Solene asked she sent that stupid birdie soaring over the net.

He forced a grin and returned the volley. Deacon liked the setup Noel had. A fine house, big ass yard, people over hanging out. It was so normal and family-like. So not resembling anything Deacon had grown up with. At thirty-two, he was over having a hellish childhood. Except his teen years had been spent learning how to kill, to gather information, to seduce a woman into telling him anything he wanted to know. No wonder he had a fucked-up social life. He could pretend all day long, but he had never felt true affection or love for a woman.

Not the way Noel and Addy clearly felt about each other. It made him feel good to see his new buddy, a guy as fucked up as Deacon, find someone to love. Normalcy was possible. Noel was proof.

Except Noel was a decent guy. He didn't steal more than a life here or there. Deacon stole dreams. He stole hopes. And he sold them to whoever Big Joe told him to.

The birdie flew back and forth a few more times before it landed between the girls. He and Hammer finally won a round, though it was too late to do them any good. The ladies declared the men lame with a capital L, and themselves the victors. Game over.

Deacon grabbed a sleepy-looking Little Dee and carried him inside. He tucked him in his crib, turned on the monitor and dragged its twin outside with him, hoping he wouldn't pick up any groans and moans through Noel's adjoining bedroom wall.

He set the monitor down and waited while Hammer lit the grill on the outside patio. *Totally killer house, Noel.*

"Okay, I'm grilling hotdogs and burgers," Hammer announced. "What else?"

"Beer." Deacon sighed, at one with the festivities. *So damn content right now.* "We need beer."

Solene surprised him by agreeing. "You got that right. This is my last night staying next door. Something to celebrate. I miss my bed."

Deacon knew this would be tricky. And fun, seeing her all riled up. His mood turned from peaceful to crafty. He grabbed a few beers from a nearby cooler and handed them out. Then he held his bottle up for a toast. "To Solene moving home."

"Cheers!" They clanked the bottles and drank.

Hammer watched him with amusement. He knew what was coming.

"And," Deacon added, raising his bottle once more, "to me going with her. Solene has some of the finest views from the island. I can't wait."

Vi and Hammer clinked bottles, Vi looking like she tamped down laughter.

Solene gaped. "*Excuse me?*"

Hammer put on a sad face. "Sorry, Solene. But the threat is still out there. Until we have all the answers, we have to be careful. Deacon's your shadow." He gave Vi a toothy grin. "I'm yours."

Vi didn't look so amused anymore.

Solene appeared ready to kill. "No. No way."

"Yes way, darling." Deacon downed the rest of his beer and set it aside. "I'm so excited for our first big sleepover. Are we sharing a bed, or will I be using one of the guest rooms?"

She swore, rather creatively, then stomped inside shouting for Noel.

Hammer blinked. "Uh, Vi, you might want to get her. I think Noel and Addy went inside for some 'alone time,' you know?"

"Well, hell." Vi put down her beer and raced after Solene.

Deacon grabbed a fresh beer and handed Hammer one as well. "Think I said something wrong?"

Hammer chuckled and toasted him anew. "Nah. You said it just right. Now let's see if you can survive her. 'Cause if you can live through the hell that blonde is planning for you, you can live through anything coming our way."

"I'll drink to that."

THANK YOU

Thanks for reading the first in my fun and exciting series about assassins. The concept of bachelors and a baby, most notably from the popular *Three men and a Baby* movie, has always seemed like a funny one. I wanted to spice that up and write about assassins trying to handle a newborn. Hence the men (and women) of Triggerman Inc. were born.

I hope you enjoyed Noel and Addy. And just wait until frenemies Deacon and Solene battle it out in ***Secrets Unsealed***! For a sneak peek, take a look at the excerpt to follow.

I love to hear from fans. You can contact me through my website. By joining my newsletter, you can get access to cover reveals, contests, and sneak peeks, as well as free books! You can also follow me on Facebook, Goodreads, Bookbub, and Twitter.

And if you liked this book, please consider leaving a review.

Turn the page for a sneak peek at Deacon's book in *Secrets Unsealed.*

SECRETS UNSEALED EXCERPT

TRIGGERMAN INC. 2

"That... I have no words. Never seen it go down that hard, that fast, before." Hammer shook his head. "I mean, I've seen some shit. But that's just brutal."

Deacon watched the free-for-all and winced when a blonde went down under the fists of her supposed friend. "Damn. Think we should help?"

Hammer raised a brow. "Are you on crack? Because that's one of the dumbest things to come out of your mouth in a while. And considering it's you, that's saying something."

"Ha ha. Aren't you the funny guy?" Deacon didn't do drugs and rarely drank anymore, and then never to excess. Men in their line of work had to be alert and aware at all times.

This new situation, working and living around other contractors, men he now called friends, felt both different and intriguing. It was like Mexico all over again, but this time he wasn't working in loose conjunction with the guys. This time they truly worked as a team.

And man, what a job it was. He grinned, watching as two redheads started screaming at the mess, then at each other. One of them slugged the other in the mouth. That had to hurt. "I don't know. I think we should do something."

"Be my guest." Hammer took a deliberate step back.

Before Deacon could act, the epitome of femininity, sex appeal, and quick-witted sarcasm entered the scene. *And now my day is complete.*

Tall, gorgeous, with honey-brown eyes and golden hair wrapped up in a ponytail, Solene Hansen made his heart race, his palms sweat, and his mind turn clean off. Being near her amplified *other* things, though. As usual, he had to work to calm his raging body.

Hammer chuckled. "Solene to the rescue."

As she whipped by them, she turned and scowled. "Protection." She snorted. "Gimme a break. You two are useless." She hurried to separate the cluster of screaming toddlers while they fought over a spilled tower of building blocks. Her new assistant, an older woman named Darcy, was already trying to break things up. Solene soon lifted the instigator in her arms and turned, making a beeline straight for them.

Hammer used Deacon as shield, and when Solene drew too close, gave him a not-so-gentle nudge forward.

Deacon stumbled. "Son of a—"

"Here," Solene snarled, though her hands remained careful as she placed the little girl in Deacon's arms. "Hold Fiona." She returned to the melee on the brightly colored play mats, separating the dueling redheads.

He froze as an adorable, grubby toddler stared up at him with wide blue eyes. Hammer's laughter wasn't helping.

Fiona patted his cheeks, her hands soft and tiny. "You're pretty."

"That's what they all say." He started to relax, in his element charming the ladies, be they three or—he considered Solene—thirty. Then again, everyone *but* Solene found him delightful.

The adorable Fiona giggled, batted her eyelashes at him, and told him all about her brother, the mean destroyer of blocks, and her stuffed animals. He nodded, taken by her innocence, wondering if he'd ever been that pure. The little girl smiled until Hammer stepped closer, then she tried to hide in Deacon's shirt.

"You're scaring her," he told his friend.

"I have that effect on women." Hammer's expression turned sly. "Kind of like your effect on Solene."

Secrets Unsealed

Turn the page to read an excerpt of *Enjoying the Show*

ENJOYING THE SHOW EXCERPT

WICKED WARRENS

"I'm sorry, but I think you have me confused with someone else."

He narrowed a gorgeous, steel-gray gaze that made her womb clench and frowned. "Honey, I don't think you understand. Apartment 306? Faith Sumner ring a bell?" Crap, he did know about Faith and where she lived. "Now we can discuss this here, with an audience." He nodded to several people laughing as they crossed the parking lot. "Or we can go somewhere private and discuss the matter...without getting the police involved. Frankly, I'm tired of being stared at."

Crossing his arms, Gage looked completely menacing, and mouthwateringly real. Without the distance separating his apartment from the Friday night shows, Hailey's normally nonexistent sexuality kicked into overdrive. Good lord, but this man was even making her mouth water.

She eyed his irritation, figured what she knew about him after several months of observation, and knew she'd never get another chance to be this close to the object of her fascination.

Nodding, she let him drag her the distance to his apartment, not wanting to appear eager. But as they drew closer to his place, she wondered at her sanity. He'd seen her watching, knew all about Faith and her friends. Why the hell was she going to entertain his questions? Then again, considering the alternative he gave her was to talk to the police, she had no choice but to take him up on his offer to discuss matters privately. With any luck, Sydney would spot them walking the distance to his wing, or better yet, see Hailey in his apartment and race to the rescue.

Unfortunately, Hailey's worries paled next to her sudden, combustible libido. God, being so close to him was like walking in a wet dream. His rock hard body enticed, demanding adulation. And not wanting to look directly into his burning gray eyes, she was more than happy to focus on his broad shoulders and sculpted delts, his corded forearms, and especially on the taut ass encased in those jeans.

She followed him up the stairs, her gaze helplessly drawn to his powerful thighs. With some difficulty, she swallowed around a dry mouth. She still couldn't believe she was accompanying her fantasy man back to his apartment. Sydney would be expecting her back with the booze, and instead Hailey walked behind Mr. Tool, caught in a firm grip promising retribution.

At his door he paused, his eyes darkening with menace. Instead of appearing scary, he only looked sexier. "Wait right here. You move one step, I'm calling the cops on you and your peeping friends."

Frozen, she nodded and waited. As if she had a choice in the matter. She could just see her name plastered over the local news. Dull and prudish Hailey Jennison caught peeping at hard-working, blue-collar stiff. At the word "stiff" she inwardly groaned. She did not need to be focused on sex around an angry, half-dressed Adonis who didn't seem to have a woman on the horizon.

He jerked his door open and pulled her inside, locking the door behind her. From what she could see through dimmed lights, he had a nice, masculine place. Up close, his apartment had more charm than she'd seen through his windows. White-washed walls framed a spacious apartment with brown leather furniture. He had oak hardwood floors, dark cabinetry that looked extremely expensive and definitely hand-crafted. His small kitchen was bright and cheery, with an apple-green tile backsplash against white cabinets. No dishes cluttered the sink, and the rest of his place looked tidy, as if he'd recently cleaned.

For a split second she wondered if he had a girlfriend they'd never seen, or worse, if he might in fact be gay. But Faith had seen him watching porn, she remembered, and unconsciously glanced toward his windows. She blinked, noting them completely covered.

"No need to give your friends more of a show than we have to," he said in a gritty voice.

She whipped her head to him, studying him warily. What the hell had she been thinking? She stood alone in an apartment with a virtual stranger, one who seemed in a pretty fierce mad as he glared at her. He towered over her, his muscles clearly outlined in the soft lighting of the room. She took a cautious step back, aware he'd locked his door, and swallowed loudly.

Seeing her fear, his scowl deepened.

Anxiety flared. What did she really know about Gage? He worked in construction, put in a full day's work, and didn't screw around, or at least he hadn't for the past three months. He apparently liked porn—she still had a bone to pick with Faith about that—and despite leaving his curtains wide open at night, had issues with being spied upon.

He took a step closer and surprised her by sighing. "Now, Hailey, why don't you tell me what you've really been doing in Faith's apartment every Friday night for the past few months."

Enjoying the Show

TRIGGERMAN INC

Contract Signed
Secrets Unsealed
Satisfaction Delivered

And don't forget to sign up for Marie's newsletter to get updates, sneak peeks, and enter contests to win books and other prizes.

NEWSLETTER **http://bit.ly/MHnewsltr**

ALSO BY MARIE HARTE

ROMANTIC SUSPENSE

POWERUP!

The Lost Locket

RetroCog

Whispered Words

Fortune's Favor

Flight of Fancy

Silver Tongue

Entranced

Killer Thoughts

WESTLAKE ENTERPRISES

To Hunt a Sainte

Storming His Heart

Love in Electric Blue

CONTEMPORARY

WICKED WARRENS

Enjoying the Show

Closing the Deal

Raising the Bar

Making the Grade

Bending the Rules

THE MCCAULEY BROTHERS

The Troublemaker Next Door

How to Handle a Heartbreaker

Ruining Mr. Perfect

What to Do with a Bad Boy

BODY SHOP BAD BOYS

Test Drive

Roadside Assistance

Zero to Sixty

Collision Course

THE DONNIGANS

A Sure Thing

Just the Thing

The Only Thing

*All I Want for Halloween (branch off)

THE WORKS

Bodywork

Working Out

Wetwork

MOVIN' ON (VETERANS ON THE MOVE)

The Whole Package

Smooth Moves

Handle with Care

TBA

GOOD TO GO

A Major Attraction

A Major Seduction

A Major Distraction

A Major Connection

BEST REVENGE

Served Cold

Served Hot

Served Sweet

PARANORMAL

COUGAR FALLS

Rachel's Totem

In Plain Sight

Foxy Lady

Outfoxed

A Matter of Pride

Right Wolf, Right Time

By the Tail

Prey & Prejudice

ETHEREAL FOES

Dragons' Demon: A Dragon's Dream

Duncan's Descent: A Demon's Desire

Havoc & Hell: A Dragon's Prize

Dragon King: Not So Ordinary

CIRCE'S RECRUITS

Roane

Zack & Ace

Derrick

Hale

DAWN ENDEAVOR

Fallon's Flame

Hayashi's Hero

Julian's Jeopardy

Gunnar's Game

Grayson's Gamble

CIRCE'S RECRUITS 2.0

Gideon

Alex

Elijah

Carter

MARK OF LYCOS

Enemy Red

Wolf Wanted

Jericho Junction

SCIFI

THE INSTINCT

A Civilized Mating

A Barbarian Bonding

A Warrior's Claiming

TALSON TEMPTATIONS

Talon's Wait

Talson's Test

Talson's Net

Talson's Match

LIFE IN THE VRAIL

Lurin's Surrender

Thief of Mardu

Engaging Gren

Seriana Found

CREATIONS

The Perfect Creation

Creation's Control

Creating Chemistry

Caging the Beast

AND MORE (believe it or not)!

ABOUT THE AUTHOR

Caffeine addict, boy referee, and romance aficionado, *New York Times* and *USA Today* bestselling author Marie Harte has over 100 books published with more constantly on the way. She's a confessed bibliophile and devotee of action movies. Whether hiking in Central Oregon, biking around town, or hanging at the local tea shop, she's constantly plotting to give everyone a happily ever after. Visit http://marieharte.com and fall in love.

facebook.com/marieharteauthorpage

twitter.com/MHarte_Author

goodreads.com/Marie_Harte

bookbub.com/authors/marie-harte

Manufactured by Amazon.ca
Bolton, ON